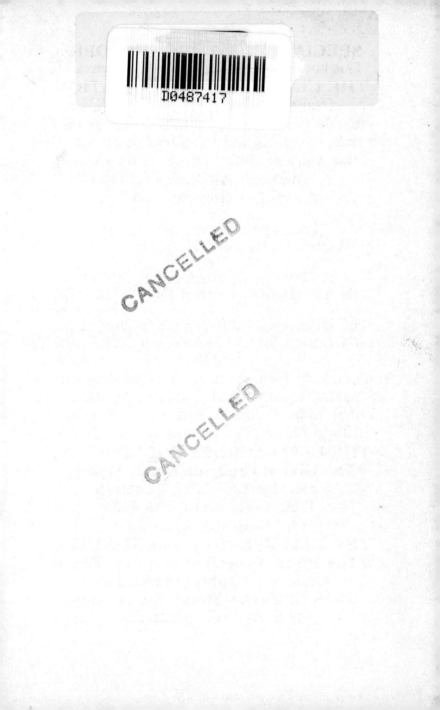

D0487417

MURDER IS MY SHADOW

LA Private Investigator Johnny Merak accepts the diminutive Charles Henning as a client, little realising the danger he will face . . . But soon, when a series of brutal gangland murders begins, Lieutenant O'Leary, leading the police investigation, is not pleased to find Johnny Merak at each of the murder scenes. And it seems that Henning had been there too! Both the police and Johnny want to question Henning — but the little man has disappeared. And the murders continue . . .

JOHN GLASBY

MURDER IS MY SHADOW

Complete and Unabridged

LINFORD
Leicester

First published in Great Britain

First Linford Edition
published 2009

British Library CIP Data

Glasby, John
    Murder is my shadow
    1. Gangsters—Fiction.
    2. Murder—Investigation—Fiction.
    3. Detective and mystery stories.
    4. Large type books.
    I. Title
    823.9'12–dc22

    ISBN 978–1–84782–638–1

Published by
F. A. Thorpe (Publishing)
Anstey, Leicestershire

Set by Words & Graphics Ltd.
Anstey, Leicestershire
Printed and bound in Great Britain by
T. J. International Ltd., Padstow, Cornwall

This book is printed on acid-free paper

1

The first murder

It was cold that October evening, cold and damp with the salty tang of the ocean biting at the back of my throat. There were few lights visible. Unlike the brightly lit areas around Sunset and the other boulevards, here the street lamps were few and far between. It was a place of dim narrow streets, empty buildings, and shadows.

I was standing in one of these shadows, watching the far sidewalk. Glancing down at the luminous hands of my watch I saw it was almost midnight. Very soon, if my information were correct, someone would be coming along that sidewalk.

I drew further back into the darkness and lit a cigarette. Dawn Grahame, my secretary, the woman who'd stood by me when I'd decided to leave the Mobs and go legit, had warned me this might be a trap.

I'd been on a number of stakeouts such as this in the past. But there was something about this one that didn't sit right with me. It was a feeling that something wasn't quite right and it made me wonder if I'd done the right thing.

What Dawn had called her feminine intuition told her that someone was out to get me and all of this was nothing more than a plan to lure me out to this lonely place. Maybe she was right, I thought, and I was glad of the comforting weight of the .38 under my left arm.

In my job as a private investigator you sometimes made bitter enemies. It sometimes happened that you upset people. Not just the big guys I'd been instrumental in sending to San Quentin or Alcatraz but also the little men. Wayward husbands I'd traced for their wives — or the other way around. Occasionally those I did manage to trace didn't want to come back and resented what I did. Even ordinary citizens could always get hold of a gun and decide to take matters into their own hands if they disliked me, and my methods, enough.

I shivered. It had begun to rain; a thin drizzle that soaked into everything. Not for the first time that evening I began to regret I'd taken this case, thinking how much better it would be in my own warm bed, or better still in Dawn's.

It had all started two days earlier.

I was sitting in my office chair, my legs on the desk. Business had been slack for the past couple of weeks. Nobody seemed to be doing anything they shouldn't. Life in L. A. was proceeding normally — no runaway wives or husbands disappearing from the marital home. None of the outfits running the show behind the scenes were gunning for each other. It seemed the bad guys were, for some reason, lying low.

But, although I didn't know it, all of that was about to end.

Dawn was busy making the coffee and it promised to be another day when little happened. Then there came a sharp knock on the door. It opened quickly and this guy came in. He paused for a moment, looking behind him and then closed the door quickly as if not wanting to be seen there.

He looked like most of my usual clients — a nondescript man, nothing out of the ordinary. He wore a neat blue suit but one that had seen better days. You would have passed him on the street and completely forgotten what he looked like by the time you reached the next intersection.

'Are you the private investigator who works in this building?' he asked.

I gave a nod. 'The name's Merak.' I told him. 'It's on the door and yes, I'm a private investigator.' I indicated the chair in front of me and he dropped into it, holding his hands in his lap.

When he said nothing, I asked, 'And what can I do for you, Mister — ?'

He looked up. 'Henning.' he said. 'Charles Henning.'

I placed the tips of my fingers together and eyed him closely. There was one thing I could definitely recognize. He was scared, running from something or someone. This wasn't the usual case of a wife who'd decided to leave home with some other guy. This was something else.

4

'So, Mister Henning, why have you come to see me?'

He ran his tongue round his lips, looking down at the floor. Looking at him I imagined a schoolboy who'd been caught cheating and was facing the principle.

'I'm being blackmailed,' he said finally.

'Blackmailed? So who's blackmailing you and, more to the point, what do they have on you?'

'I've no idea who it is. I've worked for Al Corso for about two years now — '

'Al Corso — the racketeer?'

'The same.' He sat back in the chair but he didn't relax. 'Very soon I discovered that quite a lot of what I do is highly illegal, arranging meetings for important people and making money transactions between the various outfits. Furthermore, I realized that if I wanted to stay healthy I had to keep my mouth shut about everything I saw and heard.'

'Knowing Corso and his kind, that was a very wise decision,' I told him. 'Go on.'

'About three months ago I had to go through some of Corso's private papers.

No one else was ever allowed to see them so I guess he trusted me. It was when I put them back into the safe that I came across a diary. That was when I found out that Corso was personally responsible for killing Jack Mortillo and dumping his body in the bay.'

'Mortillo.' I nodded briefly. 'I remember the case. It made front page headlines at the time. The cops never did find out who killed him. The outfits all clammed up and there wasn't even a rumour about his death.'

I could now understand why he was running scared. 'So you know it was Corso from his own diary. If you don't mind my saying so — that was very dangerous reading.'

'Do you think I don't know that? But even knowing it, I'd have been quite prepared to keep my mouth shut. After all, Mortillo meant nothing to me and even though some of my work was illegal, I wanted to keep my job.'

'Which would be very well paid,' I interrupted.

'I received what I would consider to be

excellent remuneration for what I did,' he said stiffly. 'But now someone has found that out what I know and unless I pay this guy a hundred thousand bucks he's going to slip that information to Corso. If he does that, I'm dead.'

He seemed on the verge of tears, staring down at his hands as if hoping to see the answer to his dilemma there.

'I think that's a very likely outcome,' I told him. 'But I should tell you how blackmailers operate. Okay, you pay them the money they demand but then they come back for more. They won't leave you alone until they've bled you dry. Even once they've done that they'll carry out their original threat.'

I took out a pack of cigarettes and lit one. Holding them out to him, he took one with fingers that were shaking violently. Leaning forward, I lit it for him.

Speaking through the smoke, I said, 'Surely you must realize that this is really a case for the cops — not a private investigator.'

He drew hard on the cigarette, hoping to somehow calm his nerves. 'The police won't do a thing. Most of them are on the take from the Mobs and Corso's too clever for them to pin anything on him. But from what I've heard you were once in the Organization. You know how it operates. You can find your way around the different outfits and learn things the cops could never discover in a hundred years.'

Stubbing out my cigarette I asked, 'So what exactly do you have in mind? You want me to find out who this blackmailer is and scare him off? Is that it?'

He shook his head vehemently at that. 'No — there isn't time for that. I have to pay him off. There's no other way.'

'And I presume you've got the money to do this. May I ask how you got all that dough?'

He fidgeted with his hands and I didn't think he was going to answer. But he did. 'Where do you think I got it? From Rizzio's outfit, of course.'

I'd had dealings with Sam Rizzio in the past. He ran the biggest outfit in the L.A. Underworld. From what I understood, Al Corso was his right-hand man, the hoodlum who did all of the dirty work like torture and murder.

'It wasn't difficult.' Henning went on, 'Like I said, I deal with most of the money transactions, millions of dollars. I simply siphoned off ten thousand bucks here, fifty grand there. They never missed any of it. That's just a drop in the ocean for them.'

I stared at him in utter amazement. That this little guy, now shaking like a leaf in a storm, had the nerve to fleece the Big Boys like this was something I'd never have believed.

He went on hurriedly, 'I've also got a little money of my own. I'm willing to pay you if you'll help me.'

'Pay me to do what?' I asked. 'If you're asking me to take that hundred grand and make the drop for you then the answer is — no.'

I knew that was the original idea he had in mind. Now, with my flat refusal, he was thinking fast, trying to come up with something else. Finally, he said, 'Then will you agree to be there, just to keep an eye on things. I've never done anything like this before. It's vitally important you remain out of sight. If this guy thinks there's someone else with me, he may just call the whole thing off.'

'Or if he's sufficiently determined to get his hands on that money, he may decide to finish off both of you.' Dawn spoke up for the first time. 'I still think you should go to the police.'

Henning shook his head. 'Not a chance, lady. I may just be a little guy as far as the Organization is concerned but I'm neither crazy nor suicidal. They'd be fishing me out of the bay within hours. That is, if anyone bothered to look for me.'

I reached a decision. 'All right. I'll tell you what I'll do. Have you been told where and when to drop off the dough?'

He nodded. 'An old abandoned warehouse on the edge of town. I've to be there at midnight two days from now. Here's the address.' He handed me a slip of paper with something written on it.

'O.K. This is what I'll do. I'll case the joint before you get there and then keep a watch from the shadows. You just be there

10

on time with the money.'

He looked relieved. 'Thank you, thank you.' He grabbed my hand and pumped it up and down several times before going to the door.

When he'd gone, Dawn said sharply, 'I hope you know what you're letting yourself in for, Johnny. Why on Earth did you take the case?'

I lit another cigarette. 'Curiosity, perhaps,' I said.

'Curiosity?' Dawn looked surprised. 'About some little guy who's just dug himself into a hole so deep his feet are sticking out somewhere in Australia.'

'That's right. There was something about his story that didn't ring true. He was telling only half of it and I want to find out what the rest of it is.'

★　★　★

So now I was here, standing in the shadows and getting colder and wetter by the minute. I'd arrived fifteen minutes earlier and checked out the large warehouse almost directly opposite me on

11

the other side of the street. There had once been a lock on the doors but that had long since been smashed. It had been the work of only a few minutes to satisfy myself that it was completely empty except for the usual rodent population.

There was a garage next to it but this had closed up for the night. Apart from the few streetlamps not a light showed anywhere. There was the faint sound of traffic in the distance but for all I could hear in this place it might have been on the Moon.

I reached for my pack of cigarettes; then stopped. There was a sudden furtive movement about a hundred yards away. I couldn't make out if there were one or two people there. They were just vague shapes moving in and out of the shadows but there was no doubt in my mind they were heading in the direction of the warehouse.

I knew neither of them should be Henning. If he stuck to his plan he would arrive from the opposite direction. Two minutes later the shapes vanished into the darkness at the far side of the building.

Even though I didn't like the possibility of two hoodlums turning up to meet Henning, I forced myself to relax.

I checked my watch again. It was almost on the stroke of twelve. I didn't know how long I'd have to wait but —

Even as the thought crossed my mind there came a movement on the opposite sidewalk. I recognized Henning right away. He was walking slowly, hesitantly, his head turning from side to side. He was obviously scared but somehow determined to go through with this. There was a suitcase in his right hand. It wasn't large but big enough to contain a hundred thousand dollars in large bills.

He halted when he was still several feet from the door leading into the warehouse. I saw him peering intently into the shadows. He was clearly afraid but trying desperately not to show it to anyone who might be watching.

For a few seconds he stared directly at the spot where I stood in the shadows. I knew he couldn't see me and I couldn't make any signal to tell him I was there. It was quite possible that sharp eyes, using high-powered binoculars, were scanning everything in the vicinity.

I saw him wipe the back of his hand across his forehead before walking on. The warehouse door opened as he pushed it and he vanished inside.

Now there was nothing for me to do but wait. The minutes dragged slowly as if they were elastic and Father Time had pulled them out to several times their normal length.

Five minutes went by and then a further five. The little mice inside my head were now having a wild old time, telling me that if everything had gone according to plan Henning should have been out and away long before this. It would only take a couple of minutes for him to leave the case where he'd been told and then get the hell out of there.

I waited for a further couple of minutes and then decided that something must have gone wrong. Taking the .38 from its holster I held it steady as I crossed the narrow road towards the half-open door. As I reached it I expected a fusillade of shots to come at me out of the darkness inside. But nothing happened. The silence was absolute.

Cautiously, I stepped inside. Here the darkness was even denser than outside. I could make out nothing. I called his name in a low whisper but there was no answer. I took a couple of steps forward. Where the hell was Henning? Had someone been waiting for him just inside the doorway and grabbed him and the dough before he could utter a sound?

I moved further into the building. Something scuttled away on tiny feet making me jump. My nerves were beginning to twitch and a finger of ice was brushing up and down my spine. Then I stumbled against something on the floor and almost dropped the gun as I struggled to keep my balance.

Bending, I felt around with my free hand. My fingers encountered rough cloth. Whoever it was, he didn't move. Fumbling inside my jacket pocket I took out my lighter and flicked it on.

I fully expected it to be Henning lying there — that this blackmailer had double-crossed him. But it wasn't. In the flickering yellow glow I made out a face I'd never seen before. The guy was lying on his back, his eyes wide open but he wasn't seeing anything.

Then I caught sight of the spreading dark stain on his white shirt where he'd clearly been stabbed in the chest.

Forcing myself upright I tried to figure out what to do. Did I find a phone and inform the cops — or did I do the sensible thing and get out of there as quickly as I could?

I never made the decision. There was a faint swish in the air behind me and before I could turn or bring up the gun something hit me on the back of the head and I took a dive into a bottomless pit of blackness.

★ ★ ★

How long I was out it was impossible to tell. Clawing my way back to consciousness was a painful process. My head throbbed as if someone inside it were beating a drum tattoo. Agony seared through it with every movement I made.

Opening my eyes I tried to focus them but everything seemed to be whirling around me as if I were on some out of control carousel. With an effort, I got to my knees and hung there until the place stopped circling around me. I reached out for the wall but someone seemed to have moved it.

Sucking in a deep breath, I commenced to crawl in the direction of the open doorway. There seemed to be a light flashing somewhere but I couldn't make out what it was. There was also a high-pitched wailing inside my skull; a sound that I knew I ought to recognize.

Then hands grabbed my arms and hauled me upright. A harsh voice said, 'All right, buster, who are you and what are you doing here at this time of night?'

My mouth and throat were so dry I could barely speak. Before I could get any words out, however, another voice said loudly, 'There's a body here, Joe. Looks to me as if he's been stabbed.'

'Is he dead?' asked the guy holding me up.

A pause, then, 'With a knife wound like

that in his chest, I'd say he's dead all right. It seems to me we got here just in time to get the killer.'

The cop holding my arm thrust his face close up to mine. 'Now suppose you answer my questions.'

Moistening my lips, I managed to say, 'My name's Merak. I'm a private investigator. I've got my card in my jacket pocket if you want to see it. And as for that guy on the floor I've never seen him before in my life.'

'Sure you haven't. Somebody just wandered in here, stabbed him, and then wandered off again. And you saw and heard nothing.'

There was a flash of brilliance as the second cop switched on a torch and played the beam around the interior of the building. 'There's no one else here,' he said a moment later. 'And I'd say this guy hasn't been dead more than half an hour.'

'There was somebody else here,' I croaked. 'Unless you figure I coshed myself on the back of the head. If I somehow did that, where's the cosh?'

'O.K. So why are you here?'

'A client of mine came here to meet someone. I reckon he thought he might get into something he couldn't get out of, so he hired me to keep a watch on the place while he went inside. When he didn't come out after ten minutes I reckoned it was time for me to take a look-see.'

'And where is this client of yours now?'

'That's something I'd like to know,' I said. 'After what's happened I'm beginning to think I've been played for a sucker.'

The cops both laughed at that remark. The taller guy bent and picked up the .38 from the floor beside the body. 'Is this your gun?' he asked.

'Yes, it's mine,' I said. 'I do have a permit for it.'

He thrust it into his belt after checking the safety catch. 'I don't think you'll be needing this for some time.'

'I think you'd better come down to the precinct with us,' said his companion.

'Am I being arrested?' I asked.

A pause, then: 'No, but I think you've

got one hell of a lot of questions to answer.'

Keeping my arm tightly in his grasp the cop steered me towards one of the patrol cars waiting outside and thrust me into the back before crushing in beside me. I said nothing. I needed a little time in which to clear my head and it seemed this was going to be the only way I'd get it.

Fifteen minutes later, we arrived at the precinct. The desk sergeant who took all of the details looked bored. Maybe it was the beginning of another night shift and he'd much rather be at home. He wrote down everything and then picked up the telephone and rang a number. To one of my companions, he said dryly, 'I reckon this is a case for homicide.'

He spoke into the phone for a couple of minutes and then put the receiver down. 'A couple of them are on their way,' he remarked.

They arrived ten minutes later. I'd already guessed who they might be and I knew they wouldn't be pleased to see me.

Lieutenant O'Leary looked dishevelled as if he had just been dragged out of a cosy bed. Sergeant Kolowinski seemed his usual self with no expression at all on his face. The Sergeant and I had known each other for several years and I had often wondered if, between his spells of duty and his drinking time, he ever slept at all.

O'Leary took one look at me and said harshly, 'Merak! I might have known it would be you. Goddamnit! You seem to be haunting me. Whenever there's trouble, you're always in the middle of it.'

I shrugged. 'You can't blame me, Lieutenant, if the guys I work for always get themselves into a fix. Then it's my job to try to get them out of it.'

'And it's my job to clean up your mess. All right.' He turned to the desk sergeant. 'What's he charged with, obstructing justice?'

'We haven't charged him yet, Lieutenant. He's in for questioning about a murder.'

'Murder?' O'Leary had the decency to look surprised. 'When did this happen?'

'About an hour ago, Lieutenant,' interrupted one of the cops who'd brought me in. 'We got a call to an abandoned warehouse on the outskirts. When we got there, we found a body lying on the floor. There was no one else in the vicinity but this guy who claims he's never seen the victim before.'

O'Leary heaved a sigh. 'Very well. I'll question him.' He turned and indicated I was to follow him along the corridor. Over his shoulder, he yelled, 'One of you men bring me some coffee, hot and black. I think I'm going to need it.'

Once inside the small room, O'Leary lowered himself wearily into the chair behind the desk. At my back Kolowinski closed the door and stood with his back to it. The Lieutenant took a look at his watch and then lifted his head to stare at me.

'All right, Merak, let's have it. Did you murder this guy they found in the warehouse?'

I shook my head. 'You know me better than that, Lieutenant. This guy was stabbed in the chest. If I had to kill anyone I'd use my thirty-eight. I don't carry knives with me.'

'Then what the hell were you doing out there at midnight?'

The coffee came in before I could answer. O'Leary took a sip of it and grimaced as the hot liquid hit the back of his throat. 'Start at the beginning,' he said harshly.

I sat back and told him briefly all that had happened since Henning had walked into my office a couple of days earlier. He listened attentively without interrupting once. When I'd finished, he leaned back in silence turning my story over in his mind, trying to find some flaw in it.

Finally, he said, 'So all you did was look the place over and then wait out of sight. Meanwhile this guy Henning went in with a case containing a hundred thousand dollars as a payoff to some crook who was blackmailing him?'

'That just as it happened, Lieutenant,' I said.

'So where is this client of yours now? It seems he's not around to corroborate your story.'

'How the hell should I know? I found this stranger lying on the floor with a stab

23

wound in his chest and before I could ring you somebody hit me on the back of the head.'

'And you've no idea who this John Doe is?'

'I've no idea at all. Like I said I saw someone go into that warehouse about five minutes before Henning arrived.'

'But you can't say whether it was one or two people.'

'No. It was dark and too far away.' I leaned forward with my elbows on the desk. 'There is one thing that puzzles me, Lieutenant.'

'Oh, just one.' There was a note of sarcasm in his voice. 'There are plenty of things that puzzle me.'

I ignored that. It was just his way of getting back at me for having him dragged out of bed. 'How come those cops arrived so quickly at the warehouse. As far as I was aware there was no one else around. Or was it the usual anonymous tip-off from some concerned citizen?'

O'Leary pressed his lips together so tightly they almost disappeared. He glanced up at Kolowinski. 'Find that out, Sergeant,' he said thinly.

We waited until Kolowinski came back. After closing the door again, he said, 'They say they received a call at the precinct that someone was prowling around the warehouse. Seems they take these calls pretty seriously since that place is being used by drug dealers on a fairly regular basis.'

'Was it a man or woman who phoned?' I asked before O'Leary could say anything.

'Apparently the line wasn't too good but they're pretty sure it was a man.'

'Did they try to trace the call?' O'Leary asked.

'Seems it came from a callbox about half a mile from the warehouse.'

O'Leary sat in silence for a couple of minutes. I knew his brain wasn't working as quickly as it normally did. But considering the time of night he wasn't doing too badly. He began tapping the desk with his fingers, a sure sign that he couldn't make up his mind.

At last, he said, 'All right, Merak. You

can go. Your story sounds too fantastic to be anything but the truth. But don't take any unexpected trips out of town. I'll probably want to question you again.'

'I won't, Lieutenant,' I promised. Getting to my feet, I walked to the door, paused with my hand on the handle. 'Do I get my gun back? I feel naked walking around without it.'

He thought about that for almost a minute and then nodded. 'All right. Tell the desk sergeant to give it back to you.'

I went out and told the guy behind the desk what the Lieutenant had said. He gave me a funny look but brought out the .38 from behind the desk and handed it over. I could tell by the weight that it was still loaded and slipped it back into its holster.

Then I went out into the night. Nobody had offered to drive me back to where I'd left my car. It was still raining as I started to walk.

2

Investigation proceeds

It was late when I got into the office the next morning. I'd had little sleep. My skull still hurt and the couple of painkillers I'd taken with my coffee seemed to have done little to ease the dull ache.

Dawn was already there. She took one look at me and exclaimed, 'What happened to you, Johnny? You look like the wreck of the Hesperus.'

'I had a bad night,' I told her. I sank down into my chair and propped my legs on the top of the desk.

'Didn't that man Henning turn up?' she asked, switching on the electric kettle for the morning coffee.

'Oh, he turned up all right together with the suitcase which I presumed carried the pay-off. He went into the warehouse but he never reappeared.'

'You mean he just vanished along with the money?'

I forced a grin. 'Not only that — but he left a dead body behind.'

Dawn shook her head in bewilderment. She seemed at a total loss for words but finally went on, 'Do you know who this dead man was?'

'No. He was a complete stranger. But I am sure of one thing. He wasn't there when I looked the place over not more than twenty minutes earlier. Before I could do anything else someone sapped me and just as I was coming round the cops arrived on the scene. An anonymous tip-off they said.'

Dawn pressed her lips together. 'But you think the caller was the killer?'

'Yeah, that's exactly what I think. Fortunately for me, Lieutenant O'Leary is on the case and I think he believed my story. Anyway, he let me go and gave me my gun back.'

She brought the coffee over and this time there was no look of disapproval on her face when I took the whiskey bottle from the drawer and poured a liberal measure into it.

I sipped the drink slowly. Whether it was the alcohol or the painkillers were beginning to take effect I didn't know but the pain was easing slowly. My skull still hurt whenever I touched it but I guessed I'd live.

Dawn came over to sit on the edge of the desk, her leg brushing against mine. She put her arm across my shoulders. 'All in all,' she said softly, 'this doesn't make sense, Johnny. Why should Henning drag you out there at that time of night to keep watch — and then vanish?'

She bit her lower lip. 'I could understand it in a way if that dead man had been Henning. Whoever was black-mailing him had decided to kill two birds with one stone. Get rid of him and take the money.'

I finished my drink while trying to puzzle things out in my mind. Those little mice inside my head were now having a fine old time, scampering around, throwing up questions to which there seemed to be no answers. The only thing that seemed to make any kind of sense was that Henning and this mysterious blackmailer were in cahoots.

They'd planned to skip with the hundred grand and share out the loot between them. But something had gone wrong. This third person had appeared on the scene. So the dead man was either the blackmailer — or this third guy.

I put that idea to Dawn but after a moment's deliberation she shook her head, 'If that was the case, Johnny, why did Henning drag you into it?'

'Perhaps I was to be the patsy — the fall guy. Hit me over the head once I'd found the body, phone the cops, and I'd be left to take the rap.'

Dawn got up and walked up and down the room for a moment, her forehead creased in concentration. Then she said, 'Do you know if the police found the murder weapon? Because if they didn't, where could you have hidden the knife before hitting yourself on the back of the head?'

'You're right, of course.' I jammed my hat onto my head and got up.

'Where are you going?' she asked anxiously.

'To see someone who might have some answers for me. In the meantime, I'd like you to find out everything you can about this man Henning. There may be something in his background that could help us.'

I went down to the car and drove across town to Mancini's bar. It was still early in the morning but this place never seemed to close. I needed to have a talk with Jack Kolowinski. I knew it was his day off duty and unless O'Leary had brought him in because of this case, he would be here propping up the bar.

Sooner or later, his superiors would find out how much time he spent here when off duty. I hoped, for his sake, it was after he retired and took his pension.

As I'd figured, he was there, sitting on his usual stool, a half empty glass in front of him. He was sitting in his usual pose, staring at nothing in particular.

I slid into the seat beside him and rested my elbows on the bar. He didn't look round but he knew it was me.

Finally, he said out of the corner of his mouth, 'What do you want this time, Johnny? If it's anything to do with what happened last night, there's nothing I can tell you.'

I signalled to the bartender who brought over another couple of glasses. I didn't usually drink so early but what the hell — ? If it enabled me to get some information, it would be worth it.

There were a few customers in the place, most of them looking as if they had spent the night there, either afraid to go home to the wife — or having no home to go to.

'There's one thing you can tell me, Jack,' I said softly so as not to be overheard. 'Do you have any idea who that dead man is?'

He shook his head. 'We reckon he might belong to one of the Mobs but we can't put a name to him. There was no identification on him at all.'

'Which means that this was premeditated and quite possibly he was killed somewhere else and put there.'

'You could be right, I guess. But it's up

to the Lieutenant if we start digging any deeper.'

Somehow, I doubted if O'Leary would do that. He wouldn't want to get too tangled up with the Mobs if he could help it; dead gang members turned up all the time as old scores were settled. The easiest course for the cops was to look the other way and hope that the media didn't make too much of a fuss.

I took a couple of swallows of my drink. Watching him closely over the rim of my glass, I said, 'And this guy Henning. What do you know about him?'

He rubbed a hand across his eyes. I guessed that the alcohol was already beginning to get to him. He was slurring his words a little now. 'We know absolutely nothing about him. So far, only you and your secretary have spoken to him and know what he looks like.'

'You've no records on him at all?'

'No. Not even a parking ticket. As far as we know, he doesn't exist.'

I got up. 'Thanks anyway, Jack. If you do find out anything about him, let me know.'

'Sure.' He turned back to his drink. As far as he was concerned, at that moment I didn't exist. As I left, throwing one last glance over my shoulder, I could see his pension slipping away forever.

Outside, I got behind the wheel of the Merc and twisted the key in the ignition. There was one other contact I wanted to see. Sheila Weston had been quite a big attraction in the old days when she'd used the stage name of Stella Conway. There had been talk that she was well in with the Organization at the time and they were mainly responsible for her stage success.

However, she had a good voice and almost always sang to packed houses in several of the theatres. But that was a long time ago. I wasn't sure whether she would even remember me. Even if she did, it was equally possible she wouldn't want to talk to me. Being so well in with the Mobs in the old days, she probably hadn't liked it when I pulled out and turned legit.

I took out the slip of paper on which I'd written her address. It was a number on College Street some distance from the middle of town heading out in the direction of Pasadena. I found the place half an hour later and stopped the car a short distance from it.

Looking the house over I guessed that she had come a long way down in the world since those days when I'd known her. The windows and door needed a coat of paint and there were a couple of slates missing from the roof. The small garden at the front was overgrown and far more weeds were visible than flowers.

I walked up the narrow gravel path and knocked loudly on the door. I picked out a curious shuffling sound behind it and a few moments later it opened and Sheila Weston stood there peering at me, blinking in the bright sunlight.

I'd expected to see a change in her but nothing like this. Her hair looked as if it had never been brushed for weeks, hanging limply over her shoulders. Once it had been red but now it was a sickly pinkish-grey. She wore a flowered dress that had clearly seen better days and a pair of slippers, a couple of sizes too large, on her feet. The vivid red lipstick

35

and rouge had been applied in a vain attempt to reclaim some of her former beauty.

'Do you remember me, Sheila?' I asked.

She peered more closely at me; then uttered a low throaty laugh. 'Sure I remember you. Johnny Merak. You were pretty high up in the Organization in those days, Johnny. But I've heard rumours you've turned legit.'

'That's right. I'm a private investigator now. Do you mind if I come in and talk to you?'

For a moment, a strange expression flashed across her face. Then she glanced quickly along the street in both directions before ushering me inside and closing the door. The room smelled of stale alcohol and other odours I couldn't define. All of the windows were tightly shut and the heat was almost unbearable.

Motioning me to the long couch, she seated herself in a tall, high-backed wooden chair. There was a small table beside it with an almost empty bottle on it and a glass next to it.

'What did you come to talk about, Johnny?' she asked. 'Somehow, I don't think it's about the good old days. They're long gone even if they're not entirely forgotten.'

'You knew quite a lot of the men in the Organization, Sheila,' I said. I took from my pocket the bottle of whiskey I'd brought with me. Her eyes widened and fastened greedily on it like a dog eyeing a bone.

She licked her lips. 'Sure, I knew a lot of them. But that's how it was in the old times. Everyone knew everybody else.'

'Did you ever come across a guy named Henning? Charles Henning?'

'Henning?' She pulled at her lower lip, her gaze still on the bottle in my hand as if glued to it. 'I can't recall — '

I opened the bottle and filled the glass in front of her. She made to reach for the bottle but I pulled it back. 'You get the rest when you've told me all I want to know,' I said firmly.

Nodding, she ran her tongue around her lips and muttered, 'Charles Henning. I remember now. He was the bookkeeper for Carlos Galecci's Mob. He was a pretty important guy then. Whether Sam Rizzio kept him on when he took over the outfit, I don't know.'

'He did,' I told her. Henning had never mentioned Carlos Galecci and how long he'd really been in the Organization. I recalled that Henning had told me he'd worked for Al Corso for only two years. So he'd deliberately given me the impression that prior to that he'd had no connection with the Underworld. Now Sheila was telling me he'd been associated with them for much longer. Somehow, I didn't think the woman seated in front of me was lying. It was more likely to be Charles Henning.

'I don't suppose you know where Henning is living now?' I asked.

She shook her head. 'I lost touch with him, and most of the others, many years ago. The last I heard of him he had a house somewhere on Twenty-second street. That's about all I can tell you.'

'Just one more thing. From what you knew, what kind of a guy was Henning?'

She ran that question over in her mind

before answering, then said, 'I never liked him if that's what you mean. He was much too secretive. Always kept himself to himself. Never went to any of the parties or took up with any of the girls.'

'Thanks, Sheila.' I got up and placed the bottle of whiskey carefully in front of her, leaving her to her drunken dreams of years long gone by. Perhaps they, and the booze, were all she had now.

I drove slowly along the road to the intersection, winding down the window to let in some of the cool air and then turned into the main stream of traffic. I hadn't learned as much as I would have liked and I had the feeling that Sheila had been holding something back from me. Something important.

Henning was still a mystery — someone who had just drifted into my life and now become a major part of it. I decided to return to the office to see if Dawn had managed to dig up any more on him.

There was a main intersection a hundred yards in front of me with the lights at red. Pressing my foot on the brake I turned into the nearside lane and came to a halt. From the edge of my vision I glimpsed this large black limousine draw up alongside me in the outer lane.

Maybe it was my suspicious mind or the fact that the passenger window of the other car was being wound slowly down that alerted me to danger and saved my life at that moment. Perhaps the guy in the car was just letting in some air but without thinking, I let go of the wheel and flung myself down as far as possible across the empty seat beside me,

A split second after I did so there came a couple of sharp cracks. Something hummed within an inch of my head like an angry bee and slammed into the metalwork. A moment later the car was gone accelerating through the lights. I sat up just in time to see it weaving in an out of the traffic fifty yards ahead.

There were two marks in the metal beside me where the slugs had hit the car and then ricocheted over my head. Whoever had fired those shots had clearly used a silencer and it was very possible that no one else had noticed what had happened. One thing was certain. Somebody wanted me out of the picture — and permanently.

Back at the office I found that Dawn had not yet returned. I made myself a mug of coffee with a slug of whiskey in it and was drinking it slowly when she came in.

'Did you find anything?' she asked.

'Not much that really helps us,' I replied. 'How did you get on?'

She had her notebook in front of her and began to read from it. 'There's not much to tell. It seems he started in the Organization with Galecci which means he lied to us when he said it's only been a couple of years. There's also some evidence that he's quite cosy with Malloy.'

I sat up straight at that. 'Malloy?' I said, shaking my head. 'That doesn't make sense. He's working for Al Corso which means he's in Rizzio's outfit.'

Dawn nodded. 'And Rizzio and Malloy are sworn enemies. Do you think Henning is playing a double game, secretly working for both?'

41

'If he is, it's a highly dangerous game to play.' I sat back.

Ever since the Underworld Organization in L.A. had been formed, the territory had been carved up into neat little pieces, each under the control of the various gangs. On the whole things were fairly peaceful under the watchful eye of the Big Boss, Enrico Manzelli.

It was well known, however, that Malloy wanted a slice of Rizzio's territory and Manzelli was doing his best to prevent an all-out gangland war. So just what was Henning's part in all of this?

I now began to see him in a new light — the meek little man who stayed in the background but who was really a very clever guy with nerves of steel, working for both sides.

'Are you thinking what I am, Johnny?' Dawn asked.

'That Henning is trying to play one side off against the other? That's certainly what it's beginning to look like. The trouble is that is — ' I broke off sharply at the sound of heavy footsteps in the corridor outside.

I wasn't expecting anyone but I had the feeling that whoever was out there meant business — if not big trouble. There was no polite knock on the door. It was thrust open and Lieutenant O'Leary came in. There was another cop at his back.

One look at the expression on O'Leary's face told me he wasn't here for a quiet chat. There was something on his mind and it concerned me.

'Get your hat on, Merak,' he said harshly. 'You're coming with us.'

'May I ask where?'

'You'll find that out when we get there.'

I picked up my hat from the desk. 'Am I under arrest?'

O'Leary smiled but it wasn't a nice smile. 'Not at the moment but believe me I have that in mind.'

The cop opened the door and stood on one side. As I followed the Lieutenant out, I turned to Dawn. I could see she was just as puzzled as I was. 'I'll be back as soon as this is all straightened out,' I told her. I tried to feel confident but my words sounded as hollow as a drum.

There was a patrol car waiting outside,

parked just in front of the Merc. I got into the rear seat with O'Leary beside me. He leaned forward and said something in a low undertone to the driver who merely nodded and switched on the ignition.

I immediately noticed that we were not heading in the direction of the precinct. I opened my mouth to ask where the hell we were going; then closed it. O'Leary was watching my reactions closely and I knew he wouldn't tell me our destination before we got there.

When we finally stopped we were in College Street and parked less than twenty yards from Sheila Weston's address. It looked just the same as when I'd left it only a little while earlier. There was, however, one big difference. Now a uniformed cop was standing just outside the front door, his hands clasped behind his back, trying to look efficient.

O'Leary grabbed my arm tightly as he led me along the garden path. Maybe he figured I would try to make a run for it. But at that moment I didn't intend going anywhere until I knew what had happened.

The cop who'd accompanied us opened the door and O'Leary thrust me inside. There was still that same old smell of stale alcohol in the air and everything was just as I'd seen it before — except that Sheila Weston was no longer sitting in the faded chair. She was lying on the floor in front of the fireplace, her arms twisted beneath her, her head a little to one side.

Releasing his grip on me, O'Leary grated: 'I think you'd better start talking, Merak, and this had better be good. We know you were here less than an hour ago. Two of the neighbours saw you go in and come out about fifteen minutes later. My guess is that you came here for information and when she refused to give it to you, you strangled her.'

Without replying, I stepped forward and went down on one knee beside the body. O'Leary didn't try to stop me. Her eyes were wide open, staring at nothing. She was lying face down on the faded carpet and it was then I noticed the deep red stain on one side. Touching it with my finger I held up my hand to O'Leary.

'Has the body been moved at all?'

His face was grim. 'You know the procedure as well as I do, Merak. Nobody has touched it since we found her.'

'Then if you were to turn her over, I think you'll find she's not been strangled. There are no marks or bruises on her throat. She's been stabbed just like that John Doe in the warehouse. If you want my opinion, which you probably don't, I'd say the same person committed both murders.'

O'Leary bent to check for himself. Then he straightened up and said, 'I guess that puts you at the scene of both. You don't deny you were here?'

'No. But she was alive when I left. I brought a full bottle of whiskey with me. It was more than half full when I left but it's empty now. Unless the killer finished it off, it must have been her.'

'Then why did you come to see her?'

'As I said, I thought she might be able to fill me in on Henning. She was a star in the various theatres many years ago and like most of them she got where she was with help from the Mobs.'

I was beginning to feel that tight, empty way again. A few bits of the puzzle were trying to slot themselves into place but I didn't particularly like the picture that was beginning to emerge.

I could visualize what had probably happened. Somehow, I had been tailed to this place. Someone was starting to think I was getting too close to the truth and if Sheila knew anything she had to be silenced. Just in case she had told me anything important, they'd also decided to end my snooping around with a couple of bullets at the traffic lights.

The trouble was I didn't think I'd be able to get O'Leary to believe that. Elections were coming up soon and the Mayor would be breathing down his neck, ordering him to close this case satisfactorily as soon as possible. He had a reputation as a straight cop but right now with only one suspect, Johnny Merak, he was going to lay it on me as thickly as possible.

At that moment a couple of guys came into the room. One of them said, addressing O'Leary, 'Is it all right for me to examine the body, Lieutenant?'

O'Leary gave a terse nod. 'I reckon the photographers have finished. Go ahead, doc.'

He said something in a low undertone to the second guy and then swung on me. 'Just what kind of information were you hoping to get from this woman, Merak?'

'I wasn't sure. I didn't expect much but she did tell me one thing I didn't know.'

'Oh, and what was that?'

'It appears that Henning was working for Al Corso but at the same time he was thick in with Malloy.'

O'Leary's eyebrows went up so high they almost vanished into his hair. He rubbed his chin reflectively. It made a scratching sound in the silence. 'I thought Corso and Malloy were at each other's throats. You're absolutely sure you heard her right?'

'Quite sure. And she wasn't so far gone with the drink not to know what she was saying. That's why I have to find Henning. There's something here that doesn't add up. Now he's gone to ground somewhere and — '

The Lieutenant drew himself upright. 'You'll do nothing of the kind, Merak. You'll stay out of this from now on. This is a double homicide and at the moment you're my prime suspect. From what you've told me you've done everything that Henning asked of you. He's no longer your client so you'll drop this case as of now. Got that?'

'That's not the way I see it, Lieutenant. My job was to see that he got out of that warehouse in one piece and on his own two feet. So far I've seen no evidence that he did. Until I know for certain that he's not in the sea with concrete strapped to his legs or lying in a gutter someplace, my job isn't finished.'

O'Leary glared at me. 'You're beginning to get in my hair, Merak,' he said icily. 'I don't personally care what the hell you do but don't get under my feet. And if you get lucky and find Henning before I do, you turn him over to me right away.

'I'll be the one asking the questions. I could arrest you now for a double murder and, with a bit of luck, make it stick. Now get out of my sight.'

'I wouldn't bet my pension on you getting me for murder,' I said. From the look on his face I knew the sarcasm had hit home.

The trouble was, I told myself as I went out, it was one thing to know you were innocent but a very different one to prove it.

The cop was still standing outside the door as I left. He didn't look a bit happy as I passed him. He was just staring into space, probably wondering what the hell he was doing there.

Back at the office I told Dawn all that had happened. She listened in apprehensive silence.

Then she said, 'Was this woman a friend of yours, Johnny?'

'I knew her well in the old days. She was good then, almost made it to the top. She played to packed houses almost every night in the theatres.' I sat down and added, 'No matter how low she'd sunk, she certainly didn't deserve to die like that, alone in that place.'

'No one should die like that,' Dawn said. 'But I guess that's the way it goes sometimes when you mix with people like these.'

I nodded in silent agreement. Sitting there, I tried to figure out who could have killed her — and why. Had she told me everything she knew during our brief conversation? I wondered. Or had there been something more that she was too afraid to tell — something that someone at the top didn't want anyone to know?

At that moment my train of thought was rudely interrupted by the shrill ringing of the phone. I felt sure it was Lieutenant O'Leary wanting me to come in for further questioning.

Instead it was the very last person I expected to be calling me. I recognized Henning's voice at once.

'Mister Merak?'

'That's right,' I replied. 'Where the hell are you and why did you run out on me like that?'

'I apologize for what happened that night but unfortunately, as things turned out, I had no choice in the matter.'

'No choice?' I almost shouted the words as I tried to control my anger. 'You

51

ask me to look out for you and then you skip the joint leaving me to face possible murder charges. I reckon that will take a hell of a lot of explaining on your part.'

'That's why I'm phoning you now. Do you know the Bandolero Club on Twenty seventh Street?'

'I've heard of it.'

'Good. I'll meet you there at two o'clock tomorrow afternoon. It's imperative I should talk to you so don't be late. And don't bring anyone with you.'

'I think you'd better tell me now what this is all about or — ' I stopped. I was talking to a dead line. He'd put the receiver down.

'Who was that?' Dawn asked. 'Not O'Leary again?'

'No. It was our mysterious friend, Charles Henning. He wants me to meet him tomorrow at the Bandolero Club.'

'Be careful, Johnny. It sounds like a trap to me. Remember what happened the last time.'

'I remember,' I said as I put the receiver back on its cradle. 'But I'll never learn anything just sitting here. I'll have to go and hear what he has to say.'

'Then at least put O'Leary into the picture,' Dawn insisted.

I took out a cigarette and lit it. It helped me to think more clearly. 'I'm afraid if I told O'Leary about this phone call there'd be no meeting tomorrow. Henning may look like a fool but he's a very clever man. The minute he spots anyone with me he'll be gone.'

'Then I'll come with you to keep you out of trouble.' She'd thrust her chin out and I knew she meant it.

I shook my head. 'You're the one person who can't come, Dawn. You forget. Henning would recognize you right away.'

She threw her hands into the air in an exasperated gesture. 'Then do what you think right, Johnny. But one of these days you're going to land yourself into the middle of something you can't handle.'

3

Henning reappears — and disappears

My watch said ten minutes to two as I stood on the street corner opposite the Bandolero Club the following afternoon. Through the wide window I could see that there were very few customers in at that time of the day. Most would have finished their lunch and left some time before.

The two or three seated at the tables were obviously late-day drinkers. I made out three bartenders standing idly behind the bar. Obviously there was very little for them to do and they were waiting impatiently for the remaining customers to leave.

I'd been standing on the same spot for almost half an hour, taking note of everyone who'd gone in or come out. So far there had been nothing suspicious, none of the gang members I could recognize.

If Henning was there he'd been in for quite a while and was somewhere out of sight from the street. I waited until my watch said two minutes to the hour, checked the .38 was in place, and then walked across the street and pushed open the door.

There were three people there apart from the three men in white aprons standing in a row behind the counter. None of them turned to look at me as I crossed to the counter.

One of the guys sidled along the bar and said grudgingly, 'What'll it be, mister?'

'Bourbon on the rocks,' I said casually. I waited until he came back with the drink and then asked, 'Do you know anyone called Henning, Charles Henning? I believe he's a regular customer of yours.'

A funny look flashed across the other's face. For a moment his glance flicked downward towards the back of the counter. I guessed there was either a shotgun or a baseball bat there, ready if I caused any trouble.

Then he switched his glance back to me. 'Never heard the name,' he said softly.

'No? Maybe you should ask one of your partners. If by some strange chance this guy you say you don't know should happen to be on the premises, tell him Johnny Merak is here to see him.'

The funny look was still there as he went to one of the other two guys and spoke in a low undertone. After a moment, the taller guy nodded and walked over. 'You wish to see Mister Henning?'

'That's right. He phoned me yesterday asking me to meet him here at two o'clock. Now that's exactly what my watch says the time is. So where is he?'

'Do you have any identification?'

I took out my wallet and handed him my business card. He perused it carefully before handing it back.

'If you'll follow me, sir, I'll take you to him.'

'Now that's better,' I said. Taking my drink with me I followed him to a door at the far end of the room. He knocked four times and then opened the door, motioning me to go in.

I went in and the door closed softly behind me. I immediately guessed this was a room very few of the ordinary customers ever saw or even knew existed. It was lavishly furnished and obviously a very private place. A room for some secret tryst if the money was right where no one else would know who was there. It was also a room where top gangland members might congregate for their secret meetings.

At that moment there was only one occupant, sitting in a plush high-backed chair near the ornate fireplace. It was Charles Henning. I noticed he still had the suitcase with him. It was on the floor between his feet. He had a glass of liquor in his hand and there was a bottle and an empty glass waiting on the small table.

He waved a negligent hand towards them. 'Help yourself, Merak. And thank you for coming and being so punctual.'

'I only came because I need some explanation of your actions since we first met,' I said dryly. I poured some of the spirit into the glass and sat down in one of the other chairs. It felt as if I were floating on air. 'Now suppose you tell me exactly what's going on.'

He sipped his drink for a moment before saying, 'You know that I — ah, appropriated — quite a large sum from my employers. A sum that, at the moment, they're not aware has gone. Very soon, after my arrangements have been satisfactorily completed, I shall be over the border into Mexico. There I intend to live in the style that only money like this can buy.'

I shook my head. 'You'll never make it as far as the border, Henning. You know that. The Organization doesn't allow anyone to leave. You think you're safe with that dough. Believe me, the Mobs will know by now what's happened. You won't get a mile from here.'

'I'll make it.' For some strange reason he seemed remarkably sure of himself. I had the feeling he was merely playing with me and it was a feeling I didn't like.

'And what makes you so sure?' I asked. 'A few people have tried to leave the

Organization and far fewer, if any, have ever made it.'

'I'm aware of that. You made it and I've planned all of this for some time now, down to the very last detail.'

'There's one thing you obviously didn't plan.'

He smiled faintly. 'And what might that be?'

'What's to stop me taking out my gun and marching you straight to the precinct to meet Lieutenant O'Leary? I'm sure he'd be very interested to hear your story.'

His smile widened at that remark as if I'd said something really funny. There was, however, a hint of menace behind his action. 'Take it from me, you'd never make it out of here with me. You see, all those men in here are my friends. They'd kill you before they let you take me.'

Somehow, I believed him. He was too confident for it not to be the truth. 'And you really think the Organization won't stop you?'

'By the time they've discovered what's happened I'll be out of their reach.'

'Believe me,' I said soberly, 'there's nowhere in the world where you'll be out of their reach. You might reach Mexico but they'll track you down. Your best bet would be to talk with O'Leary.'

He frowned at that. 'You're talking like a fool now, Merak. You know what would happen if I did that. They'd make me testify against Al Corso for killing Mortillo, take all of this money I've spent so long accumulating, and put me into one of their protection programmes. What kind of life is that?'

'Better than having Corso breathing down your neck, looking over your shoulder for the rest of your life, never knowing when a bullet will come out of the darkness.'

'You don't frighten me, Merak. I know what I'm doing.'

'Then if you're not going to let me help you, why ask me to meet you here?'

He shrugged. 'I just wanted to say I'm sorry I got you into all this mess with the cops. You're a regular guy and believe me I never meant that to happen. Once I get to Mexico I'll see that O'Leary gets a message telling him you had no part in these murders.'

'That's real nice of you,' I said sarcastically. I got up. 'If that's all you've got to say there's no point in me staying.'

He looked at me in a funny sort of way and then said softly, 'I do have something more for you. I'm quite sure you'll find it interesting. What you do with it is entirely up to you.' He reached into the inside pocket of his jacket and took out a sheet of neatly folded paper. Leaning forward, he handed it to me.

'What's this?' I asked.

Peering at me through his glasses, he said calmly, 'If you read it you'll see that it's the number of a safety deposit box. Once you find it and open it, there is something there which I'm sure you'll appreciate.'

'Money.' I figured he was talking about my fee, which he had not yet paid.

'Something far more important than that,' he replied enigmatically. 'But if you do get your hands on it, be very careful. I'm sure there are more people than you after it.'

'Aren't you going to tell me what it is?'

'No.' He shook his head emphatically. 'I'll leave you to find that out yourself. But you'll also need this.'

He fumbled inside his pocket once more. When his hand emerged it was holding a small key. 'This will open the box.'

I placed the key and sheet of paper in my pocket as I walked to the door. This wasn't how I'd hoped things would turn out but it was clear that nothing I said was going to change his mind.

I opened the door. I had a brief glimpse of a dark shadow standing there and then the whole world seemed to explode in my face.

★   ★   ★

Drifting back to consciousness was a long and painful process. My head hurt. It throbbed as if an entire band of drummers were beating a tattoo inside it and there was a lump just coming up above my forehead. With an effort, I managed to turn my head slightly, ignoring the agony that lanced through it with every little movement.

Opening my eyes, I tried to make out where I was. It took several moments for me to realize I was lying in the doorway of that room at the rear of the Bandolero. The silence all around me was as deep as the grave.

I lay there for a couple of minutes trying to collect my senses. Then, sucking in a deep breath, I reached for the wall and tried to stand up but that only made the spinning inside my head worse. There was only one thing I could do. I got to my knees, hung there for a while, and then pushed myself across the floor to one of the chairs.

Everything was still spinning around me. It felt as though I was standing on a carousel with the motor running out of control.

Slowly my vision righted itself. I was able to turn and look into the room around me without falling over. What I saw, I didn't like. There was a body sitting in the chair where Henning had sat and for a moment I thought it was him. But it wasn't. As on that previous occasion this was some guy I'd never seen before. He was lying back with his head a little on one side and the widening red stain on his shirt told me everything. He'd departed this world in the same way as the other John Doe in the warehouse. A single stab wound in the chest.

Glancing down I noticed that the suitcase was no longer there on the floor. It had vanished along with Henning. Clawing at the chair I somehow managed to stagger upright. I tried desperately to think logically.

Some time after I'd been hit on the head Henning had vanished again and once more a body had been placed in the room. Thinking so hard set my head hurting again. Spasms of agony kept shooting down into my neck and shoulders. Those little mice were telling me that all of this made no sense at all; that it was some kind of nightmare that kept repeating itself like a stuck phonograph record.

All I wanted to do was lie down and sleep it all away, not waking until it was all over. But with an effort I remained upright. Little fragments of memory began coming back.

Digging into my pocket I felt my fingers close around the key and piece of paper Henning had given me. Whoever had slugged me, it was clear they'd known nothing of these. Otherwise, like Henning and the suitcase, they'd have gone.

I now had two choices. I could just walk out of there and try to forget all about it — or I could phone O'Leary and go through his endless questioning all over again. In the end I decided that the latter might be the lesser of two evils..

I staggered through into the bar. The first thing I noticed was that the place seemed empty, utterly deserted. There was no sign of the three customers who had been in earlier. Then I glanced along the back of the long counter and saw the three bodies lying there. Perhaps they had been hired to keep a close watch on Henning and see that no harm came to him. If that was the case they hadn't done a very good job.

There was a phone on the wall at the far end of the bar. Keeping one supporting hand on the counter, I edged over to it and rang O'Leary's number. I got Kolowinski and told him briefly what had happened.

'Is this your idea of a joke, Johnny?' he said.

'I don't normally joke about four murders, Jack. You'd better get O'Leary over to the Bandolero Club right away. Tell him Henning has slipped through our fingers again. I'm sure he'll like that.' I put the phone down before he could say anything more.

I didn't reckon O'Leary would think my message was a joke. He didn't. Five minutes later there was the banshee wail of a siren just outside. The street door opened and he came in with Kolowinski trailing along behind him.

His face looked as if he was chewing on something nasty. 'You again, Merak.' He almost snarled the words. 'Can you never keep out of trouble?'

'I guess not, Lieutenant,' I replied.

'The sergeant tells me that Henning

was here. So where is he now?'

'That's what I'd like to know. He phoned me yesterday and asked me to meet him here at two. I figured he might want to turn himself in but he had other plans. He has everything planned to slip over the border into Mexico with the dough.'

'So why didn't you tell me about this telephone conversation you had?'

'Believe me if I had he'd never have turned up. Right now, however, he could be on his way out of the country.'

O'Leary turned to one of the cops. 'Put out a call to all border posts and airports to stop Henning,' he grated. 'Also make sure all roads are blocked.' Swinging on me, he asked, 'What's his description? So far, only you and your secretary appear to have seen this guy.'

'Small, nondescript man, about five-five in height. Wears thick lenses in his glasses. Talks with a kind of squeaky voice. That's about all I can tell you.'

'You got all that?' he asked the cop.

The other nodded and hurried off.

'You'll want to give this whole place the

once-over, Lieutenant,' I said. 'Just like the last time Henning disappeared there's a body in the room yonder. That's where I met him about half an hour ago.' I pointed towards the open door. 'There are also three stiffs behind the bar.'

For a moment I thought he was going to choke. Then he pulled himself together and turned to Kolowinski. 'Check that, Sergeant,' he muttered hoarsely.

Kolowinski came back a little while later. 'He's right, Lieutenant. Another stabbing but those guys behind the bar were all shot.'

'That's what I would have expected,' I said. 'There's some kind of ritual here that I can't quite figure out.'

'What do you mean by that?' O'Leary rapped.

'Well, we have three murders. Sheila Weston and two unidentified men all stabbed through the heart. Yet those three other guys behind the bar were all shot. Why didn't our killer just shoot the guy in that room too? Quicker and just as effective.'

'How the hell do I know what goes

through this murderer's mind?' O'Leary grunted. His hard eyes stared directly at me. 'And why were you left alive on each occasion?'

'Maybe because I live a good clean life,' I suggested.

He didn't like that. I could see that this case was getting to him and he was beginning to feel it. He was a guy who liked facts and results. At the moment he was getting neither and it galled him.

'Any identification on that guy in the room?' he asked Kolowinski.

The Sergeant shook his head.

'Damn.' O'Leary seemed to be speaking to no one in particular. 'Two bodies we know absolutely nothing about. This case is becoming weirder every day.'

'There has to be a logical reason for everything,' I told him. 'It's just that we haven't found it.'

I made to say something more but at that moment the street door opened again and this guy came in. He wore a long black coat that flapped around his ankles. His eyes, behind thick gold-rimmed spectacles, stared myopically about him.

'Where's the body, Lieutenant?' he asked conversationally. There was a thick notebook protruding from his top pocket.

'Whoever you are, you can get out of here,' O'Leary snapped. 'Right now. This is a crime scene and — '

The guy pulled out a card and handed it to him. 'Charlie Forsythe, chief reporter for the local newspaper,' he announced. For a moment I thought he was going to bow to the Lieutenant.

O'Leary gave the card a cursory glance and handed it back. 'I don't give a damn if you're the President,' he grunted. 'Now get out.'

Forsythe didn't seem in the least put out by the Lieutenant's attitude. 'You're forgetting there's such a thing as freedom of the press,' he went on evenly. 'I'm just doing my job.'

'Then leave me to do mine. If you must stay just keep out of my way and don't touch anything.'

'I will,' Forsythe promised. He turned to me as O'Leary moved away. 'You're Johnny Merak, the private investigator, aren't you.' It was more of a statement than a question. 'May I ask why you're here?'

'I came to meet someone. However, he seems to have disappeared but he left something behind.'

'Oh, what was that?' He had his notebook out, his pen poised over it.

'A dead body in the room over there.'

'I see.' Oddly, he didn't seem surprised by this news. 'And do you know who the victim is?'

I shook my head. 'I've no idea and there are no items of identification on him.'

He pursed his thin lips as he jotted something down. 'Don't you find that strange?' He glanced up from what he had written.

'Very strange,' I replied.

He eyed me shrewdly. 'I have this feeling you know more about this than the Lieutenant. I don't suppose you'd come out to my car and tell me what you do know?'

'Sure, why not? Anything to help the press. Besides, it will get me away from O'Leary for a while.'

I followed him outside. There was a car parked just in front of mine that I guessed was his. I stared at it for a moment in amazement.

It was an old black Model T Ford. I reckoned it was probably the only one still running in L.A. It looked as if it rightly belonged in some museum.

He opened the door for me and then went round to the other side, lowering himself into the seat behind the wheel. There had obviously been some major modifications made for it started first time with a key.

Swinging the wheel, he edged out into the middle of the street. I sat back wondering where he meant to take me. We could have talked just as well in the car there was nobody in the immediate vicinity to overhear us. Soon we were heading out of town into the open countryside. He sat in silence beside me, hunched forward over the wheel, peering through the dusty windscreen.

What with the dirt smeared all over the glass and his poor eyesight it was a wonder he could make out the road ahead of us. Fortunately there was scarcely any traffic otherwise I'd have insisted he stop the car and I would have walked all the way back into town.

After about twenty minutes he suddenly pulled off the narrow road and stopped. We were somewhere in the hills. 'We can talk here without being interrupted,' he said, switching off the engine.

Judging by what I could see outside I doubted if there was another living soul within five miles of us. He took off his spectacles and polished them meticulously with his handkerchief.

After a brief pause he put them back on and said, 'I think you and I can make a deal. You tell me what you know about what happened back there and I'll tell you something that might just save your life.'

'Very well,' I agreed. I wasn't sure what he meant by his last statement but I figured I'd go along with him.

I told him everything that had occured since Henning had walked into my office a few days earlier. I took it slowly to allow him to write it down. I didn't however make any reference to the key and box number Henning had given me. When he had finished he stuffed the notebook back into his pocket.

'I must admit I've never heard of this guy Henning but I'll certainly dig around.'

'So what is it you can tell me that might save my life?' I asked.

'From what you've told me it's clear that this man Henning has some extremely valuable information concerning Al Corso. In fact if that got into the hands of the Feds, Corso could face the chair.'

'Provided Henning could be found and made to testify,' I reminded him.

'That's true, of course. But somehow Corso has found out about your link with Henning and now you represent a very great threat to him. I'd say he doesn't like anything like that hanging over him. My understanding — and I have this from a very reliable source — is that he's put out a hit on you.'

I didn't doubt he was telling the truth. After all, he had no axe to grind and there was no reason for him to lie.

'So Corso wants me out of the way.'

'Permanently. My advice is to do the same as Henning and try to get out of the country, certainly as far away from L.A. as possible. These men aren't playing games you know.'

'I'm well aware of that,' I said grimly. 'I've had enough dealings with them in the past to know how they operate. And thanks for letting me know how things stand between me and Corso. I'll watch my back from now on.'

'Then you don't intend to make yourself scarce?' He seemed surprised.

'I spent more years than I care to remember in the Organization, including a three year stretch in the Penitentiary. I don't scare that easy.'

'Then on your own head be it.'

There was an uneasy silence between us as he drove back into town. Forsythe dropped me off in front of the Bandolero. Just as he drove away O'Leary came out of the club. The scowl on his face didn't make him look any more beautiful.

'Where the hell have you been?' he demanded roughly.

'Just went for a drive with Forsythe,' I told him.

'Well I want to see you at the precinct tomorrow morning. Nine o'clock. Be there.'

I knew I'd have to do as he said. One could play around with the Big Boys at times but when O'Leary said you did something, you did it without question.

I went back to the office. Dawn was filing her nails. It was what she did when she was worried. She looked relieved to see me and put the file back into its case. 'Did Henning turn up?' she asked.

'Oh sure. He was there all right, apparently all set to skip across the border into Mexico.'

'So what went wrong?'

'Everything. I got another knock on the head and when I came round Henning was gone again but he'd left something behind.'

'Not the hundred grand?'

'No. Another body.'

For a moment, she said nothing. I could see that this was something she'd never expected. Then she said musingly,

'You know, Johnny, this case is becoming more and more weird all the time.'

'There's something else.' I brought the piece of paper and key from my pocket and laid them on the desk.

'What's that?' she asked. The tone of her voice intimated that it was something that would get me even deeper in trouble.

'They're the key and number to a safe deposit box somewhere. According to Henning, who gave them to me, if I find what's in the box it'll be something important, something I've been looking for.' After a reflective pause, she said tautly, 'My advice would be to turn these over to O'Leary — or better still to one of Harry Grenville's agents. Let them take care of it.'

I knew she was right. It was the logical — and possibly the safest — thing to do. But some imp of perversity made me shake my head. 'I think I'll hold on to them. At least until I know what's in that box. The fewer people who know about this, the better.'

'I think you're going to regret it,' she said tersely. 'If whatever is in that box has anything to do with either Rizzio or Corso, it'll be your life on the line. Are you so damned determined to be a dead hero?'

I knew she was saying that because she was scared. Not scared for her safety, but for mine.

I forced a quick grin. 'You know me better than most, Dawn. Once I get my teeth into something I can't let go. Besides, there has to be some logic behind all this. I get the feeling there's something we've overlooked; something that's right under our noses.'

'And have you stopped to ask yourself why Henning gave you this key and box number?'

'I suppose he knows that so long as he holds on to them he's even more of a marked man. Where Corso is concerned he's a ticking bomb just ready to go off and blow Corso to hell.'

Dawn smiled bitterly. 'And now you're that stick of dynamite. How long will it be before your world blows up in your face?'

The phone rang before she could say

anything more. I wasn't expecting either O'Leary or Forsythe to be calling. Picking up the receiver, I said, 'Merak.'

'Jack Kolowinski,' said the voice at the other end. 'I'm ringing to give you a bit of information, Johnny. I don't know if it means much but I figured you ought to know. O'Leary doesn't know I'm calling and he'd be as mad as hell if he found out. This is just between the two of us to keep it to yourself.'

'Of course, Jack.'

'We've managed to identify one of those two dead men.'

'Which one?' I asked.

'The guy in the warehouse. We picked him out from our collection of mugshots. His name is Cal Venders. He's one of Rizzio's men.'

I whistled through my teeth. 'Then I reckon we can reasonably assume the other guy belongs to the same outfit,' I said.

'That's how the Lieutenant sees it. I just thought you ought to know. Oh, there's one other thing. Those men who were shot in the Bandolero — they were all working for Joe Malloy. He owns the joint.'

'Thanks a lot, Jack. I owe you one.' I put the phone down Dawn looked at me with an expression of mute inquiry on her face. I told her who it was and what Kolowinski had said.

'Do you think it's possible that — ?' she began.

'Go on,' I said when she hesitated. 'This whole case is so crazy I'm willing to listen to anything no matter how fantastic it seems.'

'Suppose there are two of them working together — Henning and the killer. Henning is trying to get out of the country with that money he stole and — '

'And the killer, whoever he is, is picking off Rizzio's men one by one and leaving them for the police to find.' I finished. It certainly made a weird sort of sense.

'Or for some reason, he's leaving them there for you to find, Johnny. He's got some reason for involving you with Corso.'

I felt a little finger of ice run along my spine. What she said seemed logical, so logical that I couldn't find any flaw in it.

Dawn walked over and stood beside me. I could feel some of the fear that radiated from her like an invisible cloud. All of this tied in with what Forsythe had told me that Corso had put out a hit on me and Henning palming off this key onto me.

I glanced at my watch. It was almost closing up time. 'I guess I'll wait and see why O'Leary is so anxious to talk to me in the morning.' I said. 'Don't worry your pretty head about me. I spent years with the Mobs. I know how to take care of myself.'

'Sometimes I wonder.' She took her coat from the peg on the wall. Changing the subject, she asked, 'How long is it since you last had a proper meal?'

'So long ago I can't really remember.'

'Then we'll go back to my place and I'll cook you one,' she retorted firmly. 'And I'm not going to take no for an answer.'

'That sounds like too good an offer to miss. I'll be at your place in less than an hour. There's just one more telephone call I have to make.'

She looked disappointed that I wasn't going back with her but finally nodded. 'Don't be late,' she said as she went out. 'If you're as much as one minute over the hour I'll come looking for you.'

I grinned. 'I'll be there.' I promised.

When she had gone, closing the door softly behind her, I picked up the phone and rang the New York number of the Federal Building and asked for Harry Grenville. He and I had been friends for a long time and I felt sure it was about time he was put into the picture. I knew I was going way over O'Leary's head but what the hell? He didn't seem to be getting anywhere and this might just be the nudge he needed.

Harry came on the line within a minute.

4

Ordeal at sea

'Johnny Merak, Harry,' I said. 'Sorry for calling you at this hour but something big seems to be happening here in L.A. Something that I think may interest you. It concerns a guy by the name of Al Corso.'

'Corso?' A pause, then: 'I know the name. We have a file on him here — a vicious killer if ever there was one. We'd have had him off the streets a long time ago but so far we've never been able to make any charge stick.'

'Then it's possible I may be able to help you there. A guy by the name of Henning came to see me a few days ago asking for my help. Apparently he's worked with Corso for a couple of years, money transactions and the like.'

'Go on.'

'It seems Henning is being black-mailed. Someone has discovered that he's seen evidence among Corso's private papers that Corso personally murdered Jack Mortillo a couple of years back and tossed his body into the sea.'

Grenville emitted a low whistle. 'If we can get this man Henning to testify before a grand jury that'll nail Corso for sure. You know where Henning is now?'

'That's the big problem at the moment. He's disappeared for the second time after he arranged to meet me on both occasions. My guess is that he's trying to skip across the Mexican border with a hundred grand he's stolen from Rizzio's outfit. One further point, each time he's vanished there's been a body left for us to find.'

Grenville was silent for almost a minute. Then he continued, 'I presume the police know all of this?'

'Sure. But they're completely stymied. They're having all of the border crossings watched but I think Henning's too smart for that. My bet is that he's had all of this planned for a long time and he's confident he can get away with it.'

'I see.' I knew that Grenville was thinking fast. If Corso was arrested and brought in there were too many slick lawyers who would get him off. Everything would have to be as tight as the internal revenue man on a bad day before the Feds made a move.

When he spoke again there was a decisive note to his voice. 'Thanks for this information, Johnny. I'll get word to a couple of our agents in L.A. Their orders will be to pick up this guy Henning for questioning. Just one thing, Johnny. Don't worry if you hear nothing from our agents. Nobody will know who they are, not even you.'

'Fair enough, Harry.' I put the receiver down. I knew I ought to have mentioned the box key to him but I wanted to know exactly what it was that Henning had gone to such pains to hide.

Just as I leaned back I picked up the sound of footsteps in the corridor outside. I thought at first that Dawn had forgotten something but these were not the dainty footsteps of a woman.

The door was thrust rudely open and two guys stood there completely blocking the doorway. They looked as if they meant business and this was no social call.

The taller of the two rasped, 'Get your hat, Merak. You're coming with us.' He stepped forward with a quickness that belied his bulk, thrust out a hand and whipped the .38 from beneath my arm before I could make a move. He'd certainly have made the top grade among the pickpockets of L.A.

'Just what is this?' I demanded. 'A heist?'

'You'll find out soon enough,' grunted the smaller guy. He now had a gun in his hand and it was pointed directly at my head. He waved it negligently towards the door. 'Now get moving.'

I knew there was nothing I could do but obey. They had me cold. As I walked around the side of the desk, the tall guy gripped me tightly by the arm. Not that there was anywhere I could run to. We went outside while his companion jammed the muzzle of his gun hard between my shoulder blades.

There was nobody about in the building as we went down to the street door. Even if there had been it wouldn't have made any difference. One glance at these two guys and any onlooker would turn his head and walk in the opposite direction.

There was a large black limousine waiting patiently at the entrance. I felt the gun dig deeper into my back as I was bundled into the rear while the little hoodlum eased himself into the seat beside me. I noticed he kept the gun pushed hard into my ribs. Evidently, even though I didn't have my gun, he was taking no chances.

I had no idea where I was being taken. Perhaps these men had just been given orders from one of their bosses and there was no one but the Grim Reaper waiting for me at the end of the drive.

A little while later we hit the freeway with the speedometer well above the eighty mark. We passed a couple of patrol cars but no one attempted to pull us over. The limousines belonging to the Big Men in L.A. were well known. Maybe once in a while some rookie cop might flag one of them down but in that unlikely event he was soon put into the picture. Either money would change hands, or someone higher up in the force would put him wise, depending on how generous the top guys were feeling at the time.

Soon, we'd left behind the sleazy quarter of the city; the all night bars, girlie shows and gambling joints. Now we were heading into the more fashionable part of L.A. Here the big houses were all set well back from the street, the expensive cars parked either in the garages or on the wide drives.

This was where the top people lived — the stars and movie directors from the Hollywood studios. Here, also, lived the men who ran most of the organizations, men who had a finger in all of the rackets. On the outside they appeared as respectable citizens.

They gave to the local charities, attended any fund raising parties. Solid citizens who never stepped outside of the law.

But behind this façade of respectability

lay the organized crime, the authority of the Mobs, the torture and murder. These were the men who wielded the real power of life and death over thousands of ordinary people. I'd seen it all at first hand. I'd been a part of it and knew all of the angles.

We turned into a wide street with trees growing on either side. Here, the big ornamental gates were closed. No one got in there without the say-so of whoever owned the place. Out of sight would be a couple of guys making sure this order was carried out to the letter.

Then, through the windscreen, I made out a pair of open gates twenty yards further on and guessed this was to be our destination. We turned in through them a few moments later and drove up to the front of the house, the tires crunching on the red gravel drive. Glancing over my shoulder, I noticed that the gates were already closed. Two anonymous guys were fading like wisps of smoke into the shrubbery on either side.

I recognized the place at once.

Carlos Galecci had lived here until his

untimely demise a couple of years earlier. Now it appeared that someone else in the hierarchy had claimed it. Thrusting me towards the door with the muzzle of the gun, the little guy rapped loudly with his free hand. At least, I thought, they were having the decency to let me in by the front way.

Whenever I'd been taken to see the Big Boss, Enrico Manzelli, I'd always been taken round to the tradesmen's entrance.

I was led to the very end of the corridor where a door stood open. Inside there were two guys seated behind a large mahogany table. I recognized one of them at once. Sam Rizzio, head of this organization. The other was a little runt with a face like a ferret and gimlet eyes that not only bored right through you but also held a hint of madness.

I didn't need anyone to tell me who he was. Al Corso! I knew in that moment that I could expect no favours from him. Men of his calibre killed first and asked questions later.

The door behind me closed softly and I guessed, without turning my head, that there was no one else in the room. This was going to be between me — and Corso. What part Rizzio would play I didn't know.

There was no other chair in the room so I reckoned I wasn't going to be asked to sit down. This was going to be short, but not sweet.

Corso looked me up and down as if I'd just dropped in from some other planet. Then he sneered, 'So this is Johnny Merak, ex-hoodlum and now a private investigator. You don't look much to me.'

'Sometimes appearances can be deceptive,' I said evenly.

He didn't like that and half rose to his feet, leaning forward as if to land a punch on my chin.

'Calm down, Al.' Rizzio said. 'Merak has a nasty habit of winding people up.'

Corso somehow forced himself to relax. His thin lips were pressed so closely together they almost disappeared. 'They tell me that you've been talking about me with certain people.' His voice had a hiss to it like that of a snake. 'That isn't a wise thing to do. Nor is it healthy.'

'I've spoken to this guy Henning, if he's the one you mean,' I said. 'But if you brought me here to talk about our conversations, there's nothing I can tell you. Client confidentiality, you know.'

Corso turned to Rizzio. 'What the hell is he talking about, Sam?'

Rizzio's lips twitched into a faint smile. 'He's telling you he isn't going to talk about Henning.'

'No? That's the second big mistake you've made, Merak.'

'Oh? And what was the first?'

'Getting mixed up with me. Guys like you are a cent a dozen. Nobody's going to miss you after tonight.'

'Oh, they'll miss me all right.' I said, trying to sound more confident than I really was. 'Quite a few of them. And some of them have the muscle to put you away for good. Unless you get the chair which is quite a strong possibility.'

I could see that, quite suddenly, he wasn't so sure of himself. Inwardly, he was wondering just how much I knew, who I'd spoken to, and whether this was all a bluff on my part.

He must have decided it was for he smiled. I had the feeling it was the first time he'd smiled in years but it was the kind of smile that sent a shiver down my spine. Not even a mother could love that smile.

'You're bluffing, Merak. No one knows you're here and where you're going no one will ever find you. Besides, the cops have nothing on me. They've tried to make things stick before but they were just wasting their time.'

'You think so.' I tried to smile back. 'Aren't you forgetting Henning. Once he testifies against you about Jack Mortillo's murder there's no way you can wriggle out of it.'

His close-set eyes glinted dangerously at that remark. 'Henning won't testify to anything,' he rasped. 'And now you've said too much. This is the end for you.'

I tried one last chance. 'And you reckon Manzelli is going to be pleased about killing me. I've helped him twice in the past and maybe he's not a man to forget.'

That didn't work either for he said

viciously, 'Manzelli has no part in this. There's no way he'll allow me to stand trial — that would be very bad publicity for the Organization.'

I knew he was right. There might be a deep sense of loyalty among the members of the outfits but none would be shown to outsiders. I glanced at Rizzio. 'You seem to be pretty quiet about all this, Sam,' I said. I deliberately used his Christian name. 'Don't you have any say in this matter or are you leaving it all to this cold-blooded killer?'

Rizzio spread his hands in what was meant to be a gesture of resignation. 'I'm sorry, Merak. You've been a great help to me in the past but unfortunately, where Organization matters are concerned, business is business. What Al says is true. You know too much and that's something we can't allow.'

Beside him, Corso glared at me with an expression of pure malice. He's just loving this, I thought.

Before I could think of anything else to say, Corso called out something and the door opened with a soft whisper. The two guys who'd been my chaperones came in just as noiselessly. 'You know what to do,' Corso said.

'Sure,' muttered one of the men. They grabbed me roughly by both arms and hustled me outside.

The limousine was still there, waiting, only this time it had been turned to face the gate. That, more than anything, told me that my fate had been decided even before I'd been taken inside to face Corso.

The shiver came back even though I tried to suppress it. There was no way out. Without my gun I couldn't even go out fighting and possibly take one or two of these hoodlums with me.

The gates swung open and a minute later I was thrust into the back of the car and we drove out, taking the opposite way to that we had come. I knew then that we were heading out of town, possibly to some lonely spot where a gunshot wouldn't be heard and my body could be buried out of sight.

Very soon we had left the outskirts of L.A. behind. On either side of us was just bare, barren moor and with a line of blue hills in the far distance. Then we suddenly swung off the main highway and turned in the direction of the Pacific.

By now it was beginning to get dark but the sky was clear and I could make out most of the details through the window. The narrow road passed between two wooded areas and then over the brow of a low hill. There, directly ahead of us, was the ocean.

So that was it, I thought tensely. A quick drop into the sea with lead in my pockets or strapped to my ankles and I'd be talking to the fish.

The guy sitting beside me said, 'Take a good look at the scenery, Merak. It's the last you'll ever see.'

'Maybe so,' I replied, 'but it's a hell of a lot better than sitting in the chair, looking at bare walls, and waiting for the switch to be thrown. That's what's waiting for Corso and you punks.'

'That's what you think,' he sneered. 'You're nothing. Nobody will ask where you've gone and a week from now you'll be forgotten.'

My only comforting thought at that moment was that I knew that what he said wasn't true. I wondered how long Dawn would wait after the hour was up before deciding something was wrong and do something about it. Not that there was much she could do. Probably put in a call to O'Leary but that wouldn't help. He didn't like me anyway.

My thoughts gelled abruptly. We had stopped on the edge of a narrow stretch of sandy beach. About fifty yards away was a jetty, a narrow wooden tongue that thrust out into the water. There was a classy speedboat tied up with a couple of men on board.

My captors hauled me out of the car and hustled me across the sand. Our footsteps rang hollowly on the wooden planks like some hellish bell tolling away my last minutes of life.

Forcing me over the low metal rail onto the deck, one of the guys produced a short length of rope and proceeded to tie my hands behind my back. Stepping back, he lifted the gun. 'Just in case you'd like to try and make any trouble,' he said and slammed the butt of the gun hard against the side of my head.

I hit a solid wall of utter blackness before struggling back to consciousness some time later. My skull hurt again and I was lying against the hull wondering when people were going to stop hitting me on the head. The swaying, rocking motion told me that we were now somewhere out at sea. The engines were still humming somewhere in the hazy background.

Screwing up my eyes I looked behind us. The jetty was now just visible and I guessed I'd only been out for a few minutes. Twisting my head with a painful wrench of neck muscles, I glanced in the opposite direction.

At first I thought there was something wrong with my eyes. Something hazy and indistinct lay almost directly ahead of us, blotting out the horizon in that direction. Then I recognized what it was — one of the notorious fog banks that sometimes swept in from the ocean.

The boat was heading straight towards it. Thrusting out with my legs, I managed to push myself a little higher against the side. So this was the plan. To drop me overboard and where no one on the shore would be able to witness my departure.

I fumbled desperately around with my hands but there was nothing sharp against which I could try to fray the ropes binding my wrists. The guy with the gun was watching me from a couple of feet away, a malicious grin on his swarthy features.

He seemed to be enjoying himself. The remaining three were some distance away. One guy was steering the boat with a second standing just at his shoulder. The third was standing at the stem keeping a sharp look out. But as far as I could see the ocean was empty of any other vessels.

Out here, I told myself, I could expect no help from anyone. Very soon it would be completely dark. I could imagine what Dawn was thinking — that something more important had come up and I'd let her down again.

I jerked my head up as the guy in front of me suddenly said, 'You know you're too damned smart for your own good,

Merak. If you hadn't stuck your nose into this business you wouldn't be here now. But I guess that's how it is with folk like you. You make a big mess for the bosses and we have to clean it up for them.'

'I'm sure it must hurt your feelings a lot,' I said.

The insult just went over the top of his head. He wasn't the brightest of guys but then in his business of bumping off unwanted people who knew too much, he didn't need any brains.

Five minutes later and we were inside the bank of fog. It clung to everything, cold and clammy, seeping through my clothes until the chill of it hit my bones.

'How much further in do you want me to go?' called the guy at the helm, glancing round over his shoulder.

'I'll tell you when we've gone far enough,' said the man with the gun.

'Then you'd better make up your mind quickly. There might be other vessels around and we'd be into them before we knew they were there.'

After a brief pause, the other shouted, 'All right. I guess this is far enough.'

The engines stopped and the deep silence was broken only by the faint splash of the heavy swell against the sides of the boat.

The small guy pulled himself awkwardly to his feet and stood for a moment to find his balance against the rocking motion of the deck. He kept the gun pointed directly at me as he edged forward.

'All right,' he muttered. 'On your feet and don't try anything.'

I pressed my back and shoulders against the bulwark and attempted to get my legs under me. I slumped back, watching the guy closely. He did exactly as I expected him to do. Stepping forward, he stood in front of me, the gun pointing just above my head.

Before he could move, I bent my legs. My feet took him squarely in the middle of the stomach as I kicked forward. With a strangled yell he pitched backward, taken completely off balance. I saw him hit the low rail on the opposite side of the boat.

He seemed to hang there, his arms

flailing like a windmill in a gale. The gun in his hand went off and I guess the recoil threw him even further off balance for a couple of seconds later, he'd vanished over the side.

There was a faint splash but that was all. One of the remaining men ran to the side and peered over, cursing loudly. When there was no sign of his companion, he swung on me.

'You're going to pay for that, buster.' He thrust his face right up to mine. 'Before I'm finished with you you're going to plead with me to drop you over the side.'

Before I could make any further move, he ran forward, grabbed both of my arms and hauled me roughly to my feet. I knew what was coming but there was no way to prevent it. He hit me savagely across the throat with the side of his hand. My head went back and I hung there, trying to suck air into my lungs.

The next moment, he swung a hard-knuckled fist against the side of my face sending me toppling backward. The outcome wasn't what he'd intended. My back slammed against the low rail and I went over the side, hitting the water hard. There was a roaring in my ears as I gasped for air. My instinct told me it was the water filling my ears as I went under.

I came to the surface for the first time, spluttering and gasping. The roaring noise was still there but this time it seemed oddly different as if it came from somewhere in the distance. The boat was still there, motionless in the water except for the slight bobbing motion of the swell.

I just had time to notice one of the figures on the deck suddenly clutching at his chest as if he'd suffered a sudden heart attack. He went down in the same instant that I did, down into the ocean. Everything was a confused riot of noise. Whether it was the water or the blood pounding through my temples I didn't know.

Kicking wildly with my legs, I pushed my way back to the surface. They say that once you go down for the third time you're knocking on the Pearly Gates and you stay down. Just then I could almost hear the guy with the scythe whispering my name in my ears.

I tried to yell out as I came up again but the salt water had got into my throat and only a hoarse croak came out. A wave suddenly caught me and smashed me against the side of the boat. My skull hit it with a crash and for the second time that night I slid into that deep, never-ending darkness.

The slow climb back to consciousness took me quite a while. A light kept flashing in my eyes and I was shivering violently. Everything around me was a vague blur in which ghostly shapes seemed to move but nothing made any sense.

Then a voice came out of the darkness and said, 'I reckon he's coming round now. It seems we got him out just in time. Another couple of minutes and he'd be a goner.'

It was a voice I'd heard before; one I knew I should recognize. But the face bending over me seemed to waver and blur like fog. My eyes wouldn't focus properly. Rolling onto my side I coughed violently, bringing up salt water that dribbled down the side of my face. With a sense of surprise I realized my hands were no longer tied behind my back.

With an effort, I got them under me and pushed myself to my knees. I hung there for a full minute before reaching out and trying to grab something, anything substantial I could hold onto.

'Just take it easy, Johnny,' said the same voice. 'You'll be fine in a little while but you've had a lucky escape.'

'Where the hell am I?' Somehow I got the words out.

'You're on board a coastguard vessel.' Another voice this time.

'Coastguard?' I mumbled the word as if it didn't make sense. 'How — ?'

With an effort, I managed to stand and focus my vision on the men standing around me. I immediately recognized the first guy who had spoken. Charlie Forsythe! But what the hell was he doing here?

He took my arm. 'I reckon you'd better sit down, Johnny, before you fall down.'

I did as I was told. Turning my head, I glanced towards the speedboat. It lay just off our starboard bow. Two bodies were lying on the slightly canted deck. There was no sign of the fourth guy.

'What happened?' I asked Forsythe.

'I've been keeping an eye on you all day, expecting something like this to happen. I was parked in the street opposite your office when those two punks went in and came out with you a couple of minutes later.

'When they drove off, I decided to follow them and once they took you into Corso's place I didn't need the brains of a rocket scientist to guess what was about to happen.

'Once I'd trailed them to the beach I figured it was about time I called in a favour that the coastguard owed me. It didn't take us long to find you. The guys on the boat yonder decided to fight it out to the end. When there was no sign of you we guessed you'd gone overboard and luckily we spotted you before you ended up as fish bait.'

'I guess you saved my life, Charlie,' I said gratefully. 'I owe you one.'

He nodded. 'We'll talk about that later.

Now we have to get you back on dry land and out of those wet clothes before you catch pneumonia.'

I sat there and watched as two of the crew boarded the speedboat and prepared to take it back to land. Then we moved away, out of the dense fog and into much clearer air. Fifteen minutes later we docked. Forsythe preceded me down the gangway and led me to where his car was parked by the side of the road.

'I'll drive you back to your place,' he said, 'if you'll give me directions.'

I shook my head. 'I'm already late for a date.' I told him. I gave him Dawn's address. 'If you'll take me there I'd be very grateful.'

'No sooner said than done,' he remarked cheerfully, staring at me owlishly through his spectacles. 'It isn't wise to keep the lady waiting, though it might be better if you changed out of those wet clothes first.'

'I think she'll understand,' I said. 'She's that kind of woman,' I didn't know how true that was but I knew she'd be worried at my not turning up on time.

A quarter of an hour later I turned up, dripping wet, on Dawn's doorstep. She opened the door and stood for a moment staring at me. Then she found her voice. 'Johnny! What on Earth has happened?'

'Sorry I didn't get here on time, Dawn,' I replied. 'But I went fishing — only I happened to be the bait.'

I raised my hand to Forsythe as he drove away and then followed her inside. She closed and locked the door before leading me into the front room. There was an electric fire against the far wall and the warm glow reached me from across the room.

'I'm afraid I'm ruining your best carpet,' I said, glancing down at my sodden clothes.

She went into the bedroom and returned with a vivid red dressing gown. 'Get out of those wet clothes right away,' she said firmly. 'Then you'll tell me why you didn't keep our date tonight. If you only knew how worried I was when you didn't turn up on time.'

She stood before me and I could swear there were tears in her eyes. Then she turned away while I divested myself of my clothes and put on the dressing gown.

When we were seated in front of the fire, she said, 'I'm afraid the dinner is ruined. I'll rustle up something else.'

'After what I've been through tonight I'm sure it'll be fine.' Some of the warmth and feeling were coming back — and the bourbon helped too.

I told her all that had happened while we ate. The food was good considering it had been made straight from the freezer only fifteen minutes earlier. Pushing my empty plate away I lit a cigarette and offered one to Dawn.

Blowing smoke into the air, she said, 'So now you have the cold stark facts, Johnny. Corso is after your blood and he won't stop until he gets it. What are you going to do? My advice would be to get out of the country and stay out until all of this blows over — if it ever does.'

'That wouldn't solve anything, Dawn. I know how these people work. Hellfire! If only I could get my hands on Henning and hand him over to the Feds. He's the key to all of this. I'm sure of it.'

'Do you think Corso's after him too?' Dawn looked at me over the rim of her glass.

'After what he's done? My guess is that Corso wants him more than he wants me.'

'Then someone must be hiding Henning. Twice he's been spirited away from under your nose. I'm pretty sure he's in with a Mister Big.'

I cursed myself for not having recognized that before. Dawn was right. Henning might be good at figures but when it came to outwitting the Organization he was a complete novice. I turned over the various big names among the outfits.

The only one that came to mind was Joe Malloy. He had already provided Henning with a safe haven at the Bandolero — although in the end it hadn't turned out to be as safe as Henning had hoped. Furthermore, those men at the club who'd been shot were all Malloy's henchmen.

'I think you're right, Dawn,' I said finally. 'And I think I know who he is — Joe Malloy.'

110

Dawn threw me a startled glance as she stubbed out her cigarette. 'You are not thinking of asking him, are you?'

'Why not? If he finds out that the Feds are after Henning, he'll drop him like a hot chestnut.'

'Are you completely out of your mind, Johnny? Do you want to have both Corso and Malloy breathing down your neck? I think that ducking in the ocean has affected your sanity.'

'Maybe you're right. But at the moment I can't think of anything else.'

Dawn sighed. It was a small sound in the stillness. Then she got to her feet. 'Finish your drink, Johnny. Right now, I think that all you want is a good night's sleep. Just to be ready to face the Lieutenant in a few hours' time.'

She gave me that wonderful meaningful smile as she turned in the direction of the bedroom door.

5

Secret of the box

Precisely at nine o'clock the following morning I was standing in front of the desk in the local precinct. I'd noticed Kolowinski come in but he'd gone off somewhere and there'd been no chance to have a word with him before meeting O'Leary. I was hoping he might come back before the Lieutenant arrived but O'Leary turned up a minute before nine.

He saw me standing there like a lost sheep and motioned me to follow him into his office. Seating himself behind the desk, he pointed towards the chair in front of him. I sat down and waited, wondering what was coming next.

He riffled through a sheaf of papers before turning his attention to me. 'I've been going through your statements, Merak,' he said dryly, 'There are some things I don't understand and I'm hoping you can clear them up for me.'

'I'll certainly do my best, Lieutenant,' I said.

'What kind of connection do you have with this guy, Corso?' He shot the question at me, possibly expecting me to be taken by surprise. If he did, he was disappointed. I managed to keep a straight face as I replied. 'I've no connection at all with Corso.'

Inwardly, I wondered how much he knew about my close shave with death out in the bay.

'That isn't what I've been told.' He placed the tips of his fingers together and stared hard at me. 'According to the coastguard they received a message that the crew of a boat were acting suspiciously about three miles off the coast last night. When they arrived on the scene there was some kind of gun battle and someone was pulled out of the water with his hands tied behind his back.'

He paused at that and leaned back in his chair. 'That wouldn't have been you, would it, Merak?'

I knew it wouldn't help me to lie.

O'Leary wasn't the kind of guy you lied to and hope to get away with it.

'All right, Lieutenant. I'll tell you what happened. It seems that by taking on this fellow Henning, I've upset one or two of the gang leaders. Corso is one of them because Henning works for him and he reckons my client might have talked too much and told me something he shouldn't.'

'Go on.'

'Well, you know how these racketeers treat anything like that — the usual method. Even if the guy in question knows absolutely nothing, they'll fill his pockets with lead bars and drop him into the ocean.'

'And did Henning tell you anything that might give them the idea you could be some kind of threat to them?'

'Believe me, Lieutenant, I've gone over everything Henning told me. All he wanted was for me to keep an eye on events while he paid off some guy who was blackmailing him.'

O'Leary pondered that for a full minute. I had the feeling he knew I was lying through my teeth but he couldn't prove it.

He tried another approach. 'Don't you find it strange that every time Henning vanishes he's just been talking to you? Also,' he paused before continuing, 'each time it happens you're coshed and see nothing.'

'Coincidence, Lieutenant?'

'Like hell it is. I don't believe in coincidences any more than you do. There's something going on between you and Corso and as sure as God made little green apples, I'm going to get to the bottom of it.'

At that moment, there was a knock on the door and Kolowinski came in. He placed a photograph on the desk in front of the Lieutenant.

O'Leary studied it for a moment, then nodded. 'Perhaps you'd like to know that we've now identified those two John Does we found. Cal Venders and Herb Smalenski. Both are tied in with Sam Rizzio.'

I noticed the Sergeant's warning look and managed to look suitably surprised.

'And Corso is also working with Rizzio,' I said.

'Exactly. So someone has a grudge against Rizzio and is bumping off his men one by one.'

'I couldn't agree with you more.'

'So if it isn't you — and somehow I don't believe it is — you stay off this case as of now. Got that?'

'And if Henning should get in touch with me again?'

'You inform me at once and don't go sallying off to meet him unless I'm with you.'

I shrugged. 'I'll go along with that, Lieutenant,' I said.

'You'd better.' There was a hard warning note to his voice. 'I can always have your licence revoked.'

With that threat ringing in my ears, I left. I'd already decided my next move and since it didn't directly concern Henning, I figured I wasn't lying to O'Leary. My conscience was clear but those little mice inside my head were still throwing up problems that I couldn't ignore.

All right, I had this key and box number but the safety box could be anywhere. Henning hadn't given me a single clue as to its location. There were several places in the city where it could be. The railroad station, the bus depot — or maybe even one of the banks. It was going to be like searching for the proverbial needle in a haystack.

I decided to try the main railroad station first. Certainly there'd be plenty of people around but folk would be using the boxes all the time so I shouldn't arouse too much attention or suspicion.

That put the little mice to bed for the time being but there was still one thing I had to consider. Corso might be a punk and a born killer with about as many brains as a catfish but Rizzio was one hell of a clever guy with a sharp eye for any detail pertaining to the Organization.

The fact that he'd done nothing to prevent Corso from getting rid of me proved that he'd do anything to prevent Corso ever coming to trial. That wouldn't be good for the outfit's image, especially if Corso were found guilty.

If there was incriminating evidence inside this safety deposit box, and he suspected Henning had somehow obtained it, he'd put two and two together and come up with the same answer as Henning. He'd make sure there were men watching every place it was likely to be.

This wasn't going to be as simple or as easy as I'd first figured. The railroad station was, as always, crowded. I looked around. The deposit boxes were all in a long row at the far end of the concourse. A few people were there, stashing items inside them.

I watched closely knowing that somewhere among this crowd there could be a guy with a gun, possibly with a silencer fitted, ready to take me out if I made to open one of those boxes. It didn't take me long to pick someone out.

There were two men standing next to the line of telephones. One had a newspaper in his hands. It was open but he wasn't reading it, looking for the best horses in the afternoon races. His eyes were roving everywhere, missing nothing, and both men had tell-tail bulges beneath their left arms. At intervals one would say something out of the corner of his mouth to his companion.

Your ordinary citizen would almost certainly miss these small details: These guys weren't here to go on some train journey or meeting their maiden aunts from San Francisco. They were here for a purpose — and that purpose was to eliminate me before I could cause any more trouble.

Once the smaller of the two glanced in my direction and I had the feeling he looked at me longer than he would at a complete stranger. Maybe it was my imagination or I was getting paranoid. But in my business, and knowing the Organization, little things like this make you think.

I made myself as unobtrusive as possible, lit a cigarette, and studied them closely. At first sight there was nothing out of the ordinary about them. One was tall, square-shouldered, the other smaller and thin with hardly any meat on his bones. Both wore soft, wide-brimmed hats pulled well down over their faces.

They were a type I'd seen many times before — hoodlums of the lowest breed. These were men who did the dirty work for the Big Bosses.

I felt in my pocket for the key. It was still there and I'd memorized the box number. I moved as inconspicuously as possible through the crowd furthest away from my two suspects. Reaching the deposit boxes, I threw a swift glance over my shoulder.

Both of the men had gone. Maybe, I reasoned, they had just been waiting for a train or someone to arrive. Or maybe they'd split up and were much closer to me, watching to see what I would do.

I moved slowly along the line of boxes until I came to the one with the number Henning had given me on it. Inserting the key, I turned it slowly. It didn't open. Either it was the wrong box or Henning had lied to me.

Disappointed, I turned away and in that split second something smacked into the metal an inch from my head. I heard the thin screech of the ricocheting slug a moment later. There had been no sound of a gunshot. Whoever it was had taken the precaution of using a silencer.

Ducking swiftly, I doubled over and ran for the exit. Big trouble was about to break and I wanted out of it. There was the sound of shouting behind me. I threw a swift glance over my shoulder. I hadn't been wrong. My two friends were running after me, pushing aside anyone who got in their way.

One woman fell to the ground screaming at the top of her voice. Others were staring after me wondering what was happening. Ten seconds later I reached an exit. There was a flight of stairs and I went down them two at a time.

The door at the bottom opened out onto the street a short distance to the right of the main entrance. I stepped outside and then ran to where I'd parked the Merc. More confused shouting broke out behind me and I knew the two killers were still on my tail.

The parking lot was packed. Keeping my head down, I ran between the rows of automobiles. Two more slugs came after me, ricocheting off the car roofs. Pausing for a moment, I took out the .38 and lifted my head slowly. My pursuers were about a hundred yards away, running through the parking lot entrance.

Aiming swiftly, I squeezed the trigger twice. One of the guys suddenly threw up his arms as if he were trying to grab the clouds and then went down. His companion hesitated and then came on at a run.

Clearly, he had his orders and wasn't going to be scared off. Thrusting the gun back into its holster, I ran on, hoping that the Merc hadn't been blocked in making it impossible for me to get away.

Fortunately there was nothing in front of me. Sliding behind the wheel I turned the key in the ignition. The Merc was a warm-hearted creature in spite of its age and started at once. I headed towards the exit, keeping my eyes open for the hoodlum.

Then, without warning, he ran out from between two cars, right in front of me, the gun held in both hands, levelled at me. There was nothing else for me to do. I pushed my foot down hard on the accelerator. Through the windscreen I saw the look of sheer terror on his face as I gripped the wheel tightly and pulled my head to one side.

Two things happened in a single instant. The slug smashed through the windscreen and scorched past my left cheek. At the same time the bumper hit the guy before he had time to move. I saw him flung high into the air, the weapon falling from his hand.

I figured he must have been dead before he hit the roof of the Merc and then slid off behind me. I didn't stop to give him the last rites. Cutting into the traffic I headed towards the road leading out of town. I had a lot of thinking to do.

Very soon, news of the shooting would get back to Lieutenant O'Leary and there were also two dead bodies around that had to be accounted for. Those would undoubtedly be Corso's concern. Neither he nor the Lieutenant was going to like this one little bit.

I finally parked in a narrow side street. Now I was absolutely certain that Corso knew this damning piece of evidence had been taken. Since Henning was the guy who did all of the paperwork, he'd be the first Corso would suspect. So now there were four people after the little guy — Corso, O'Leary, Grenville and myself.

There were a lot of big freight trucks hauling their way slowly up the hill once I left the suburb behind. Finally, however, I reached the narrow turn off at the summit. This was no more than a rutted dirt track, seldom used by anyone, apart from a few courting couples, and I didn't expect to be interrupted.

I pulled a little way off the track and stopped, parking the Merc behind a long screen of bushes. Switching off the ignition I lit a cigarette and wound down the window. The feeling of utter frustration in my mind was beginning to rankle.

Those two killers had known exactly who they were looking for. Whether they had recognized me or not, the fact that I had tried the key in that box had been sufficient for them to act.

That was the one certain thought that crystallized in my mind at that moment. Every single place where Henning's safety deposit box might be located was being watched. Corso was taking no chances. Whatever was hidden inside it must be dynamite.

Taking a deep draw on the cigarette, I tried to put myself into Henning's mind. If this item were so damned important, he'd conceal it in the last place Corso would think of. So where in hell would that be?

In a bank deposit box? That was possible but these people often asked for some kind of identification and my possession of the key and box number might not be enough. Henning would surely have considered that when he had given the key to me.

Another alternative would be one of the main bus depots. I leaned back, finished my smoke, and tossed the butt out of the window. A little nagging idea was nibbling away at the edges of my mind and I tried to concentrate on it, to bring it out into the open.

Then it hit me. The airport! Henning was going to attempt to flee the country to Mexico. He'd realize, of course, that his chances of making it across the border were so negligible as to be almost non-existent. But he had that case with him containing a hundred grand. Maybe he'd decided to use some of it to hire a private jet and escape by air. That way he'd have a much better chance of making it.

The more I thought about it, the more logical the idea seemed. That place would be under constant surveillance by some of Corso's men, of course. But it seemed my only chance of getting to the bottom of this mystery.

I started the car and reversed onto the track. Now that I'd made up my mind I wanted to get this part of the job done as quickly as possible. I knew Dawn would be back at the office, wondering what the hell had happened to me.

It was unlikely that news of the killings at the railroad station had hit the news but in L.A. something like that travelled fast and she'd almost certainly connect me with it. Perhaps O'Leary and Corso would do the same and the former wouldn't hesitate to put out an all cars alert for me.

I gunned the Merc down the slope, the tires skidding dangerously on the soft surface. Fortunately there was now little heavy traffic heading in my direction and I made good time back into the city. I cut through the streets, heading towards the outskirts and the airport.

I hit the freeway fast, weaving in and out of the traffic. This was always heavy near the airport with people flying out of and into L.A. every hour of the day. Although I spotted no patrol car, I knew that any of the others could belong to the Organization and the Merc stood out like a sore thumb from the rest of the cars.

The parking lot was nearly full but I managed to find a space at the back some distance from the entrance. I mingled with the crowd as I went in. There were long lines of queues in front of the checking in desks but I ignored these. It was the guys standing alone, or just two of them together, who interested me — those who tried not to stand out from the others.

A couple of young children ran past me, shouting excitedly. They linked up with their parents a short distance away and the man began walking towards the deposit boxes along the far wall. Lengthening my stride, I tagged along beside him.

He turned his head to give me a quick glance, then looked away and walked on. I spotted the one with Henning's number on it right away.

An innocent looking metal box but possibly one containing something that could blow much of the Organization apart.

This would have to be done quickly, I decided, before any of the Mob who might be present could make their move. Out of the edge of my vision, I scanned those people in my vicinity but noticed nothing suspicious.

Inserting the key, I turned it. I held my breath as I pulled the handle; then let it go slowly as the door swung open. At first, I thought it was empty. Then I noticed the small brown package inside.

Taking it out, I relocked the box and moved quickly away, thrusting the package into the inside pocket of my jacket. I expected a repeat of what had happened at the railroad station, but nothing happened. So far, everything seemed normal.

Pushing my way through a jostling crowd of people entering the terminal, I went outside, scarcely able to believe my luck. Had Corso somehow overlooked this possibility?

It didn't seem possible but I didn't intend to hang around to find out. I felt the urge to run towards the waiting car but pushed it down. Forcing myself to walk slowly, I moved between the lines of parked cars, anticipating a shot at any moment.

Opening the car door, I slid into the seat. It was as I made to close the door that this big guy popped up from nowhere. He had a gun in his hand and he thrust it into the car, holding the side of the door with his other hand.

'Just give me that package, Merak,' he rasped harshly, 'and you might just live a little longer.'

'Package?' I said innocently, hoping to buy a little time.

'Don't play games with me. I saw you take it from that deposit box and I'll give you three seconds to hand it over or — '

I acted out of pure instinct. My fingers were still clasped tightly around the door handle. Before the thug could finish his sentence I pulled the door shut, trapping his wrist. I guess it must have crushed the bones almost to pulp for he let out a scream of agony. The gun dropped from his fingers onto the floor of the car.

I meant to get out of there in case there were others like him around but I didn't want to take him with me running alongside the car with his hand stuck in the door. Thrusting the door open, I swung my clenched fist at his exposed neck.

He went over backwards, clutching his hand. Blood was beginning to trickle down between his fingers. Slamming the door shut I twisted the key in the ignition. I left him sitting there. He was moaning deep in his throat, rocking back and forth, his face twisted into a tight mask of pain.

I knew it wouldn't be long, even in his

present condition, for him to get to a phone and contact whoever had sent him. Now the hunt for me would really be on. I decided to head back to the office. Maybe it was a mistake but somehow I figured that might be the last place they'd expect me to go.

I got there twenty minutes later. Dawn was seated in her chair, going through some notes she had written. Even though I was in one piece with no outward signs of being in trouble, she still had that worried expression on her face.

'What happened, Johnny? O'Leary has been on the phone three times asking where you were. He said something about two men being shot at the railroad station.'

'I'll explain later, Dawn.' I said, sitting down. 'First I want to see what Henning hid in his deposit box because that's what all of this is about.'

I took the package from my pocket. There was nothing written on it. It was addressed to no one. Pulling off the brown paper wrapping, I took out the small book.

'What is it, Johnny?' Dawn asked as I uttered a low whistle. She glanced over my shoulder.

'It looks like a diary,' I said, thumbing through the pages. 'It's one for two years ago and — '

I guess the same idea hit us both at the same time. 'Corso's diary for the year that Jack Mortillo was murdered,' Dawn said in a low, almost frightened, whisper.

I nodded. 'I wouldn't have believed that Henning would have had the guts and audacity to steal this.'

'But why do it?' Dawn asked. 'Unless he intended to blackmail Corso, maybe threaten to turn it over to the Feds if he didn't pay up.'

'Somehow, I doubt if he had that in mind. If you tried to blackmail the Big Men in the Organization you'd be signing your own death warrant. I've seen it happen in the old days and you can take it from me it isn't a very pleasant death.'

'Then why?'

'I'm guessing here, Dawn. Perhaps he figured it as some kind of insurance policy. Just so long as it remained hidden, he reckoned he was safe when he took that dough. If they found out he had all that money, he'd hope to make a deal with them.

'They let him get out of the country and in return he'll let them know where the diary is. Only that plan didn't go as he'd hoped. Someone found out and he ended up being blackmailed.'

'And we still don't know who this mysterious blackmailer is.'

'That's true,' I agreed. While we had been talking, I had been flicking through the pages until I found the one I wanted.

Dawn stood behind me with her hands on my shoulders. 'Have you found anything that could incriminate Corso?'

I gave a quick nod. 'Too damned right I have.' I uttered a low whistle. 'Listen to this. Today, I finished Mortillo once and for all. The fool believed me when I told him I was stepping down and my job was his if he wanted it. He even came alone to the Marina at eleven this evening.

'By the time he realized it was a trap he was in the warehouse and tied down in the chair. That was when the fun started although he didn't seem to enjoy it. When I'd finished with him he was squealing like a stuck pig, pleading with me to let him go, swearing he'd return to Sicily and never come back.

'Did the fool think I'm as much of an idiot as he is? Once I'd shot him in the head and taken him out into the bay it took me only ten minutes to fill his pockets with lead and drop him over the side. Even if the cops do find him there's nothing to tie me to his death.'

I closed the diary and placed it carefully on the desk in front of me. Dawn's eyes were wide and there was an expression on her face I couldn't analyze.

Finally, she murmured, 'What do you intend to do with this evidence, Johnny? I'd say it's pure dynamite. O'Leary should take it and — '

I shook my head. 'Not O'Leary.' I told her emphatically. 'This has to go straight to the Feds and there isn't much time. It's possible they trailed me here and if they did we're both in danger.'

I picked up the phone and rang the number of the Federal Building in New

York. Fortunately, I got through almost at once. It was Grenville who answered.

'Johnny Merak, Harry,' I said. 'This is important. I've got Corso's two-year-old diary right in front of me. He describes in some detail how he finished off Jack Mortillo. Everything is in his own hand writing.'

For a moment I thought the news had rendered him speechless. Then he said, 'Does Corso have any inkling of this, Johnny?'

'I'm afraid so. I've had punks on my tail all day and unfortunately I had to kill two of them.'

'Where are you now?'

'In my office.'

'Not the safest place as you probably realize. And I presume Dawn is there with you.'

'Yes, she's right beside me.' I could visualize him staring down at the phone in his hand wondering what was the best thing to do.

Then he said urgently, 'Put the phone down, Johnny. I'll get in touch with our two agents in L.A. right away. They'll be at your office within ten minutes. Give that diary to them. With that evidence we can move in on Corso right away and somehow, I don't think any slick city lawyer will get him off the hook this time.'

'Just one thing, Harry. How will I know my visitors are the real McCoy?'

'Their names are Peter Kendall and Alan Maisfield. They'll have identification and they'll use the code word Henning.'

'I understand, Harry.' I put the phone down and sat back. I glanced at Dawn. 'A couple of Federal agents should be here within ten minutes. In the meantime I think you should leave, just in case Corso's boys get here first. I'll check that the coast is clear and — '

'I'm not going anywhere, Johnny.' There was a defiant note in her voice.

'Don't be a fool, Dawn. There won't be one of them this time and they don't treat women any differently to anyone else who gets in their way.'

She thrust her chin out. 'I told you when we first met that these hoodlums don't scare me — and I meant it. You've got another gun in your drawer. Just give it to me. I know how to use it.'

'I know you do but this is no time for heroics and — '

She stood her ground and held out her right hand. 'Give it to me, Johnny.'

I knew then that it was pointless to argue with her. Opening the drawer, I took out the Luger I'd had for more than ten years. It was a weapon I'd never registered; a relic of the old Organization days. That constituted a felony, of course, if the cops ever found out. So far, they hadn't.

I checked that it was loaded and the safety catch on and then gave it to her. 'If you do have to use it,' I went on, 'be careful. The recoil of that weapon can break your wrist.'

'Don't worry about me. I've used a heavy gun like this before. My Daddy taught me how a long time ago.'

I walked over to the window and peered out, pressing myself hard against the wall. The street below was empty except for a couple of parked cars and a man and woman walking slowly past on the sidewalk.

I was beginning to feel the tension now. The atmosphere inside the small office was like that just before a thunderstorm broke. I wondered if Grenville had got in touch with his men, how far away they were when they got the message — and if they knew exactly where my office was situated. All of these details were racing through my mind building up into one big question mark.

I had a vision of sleek black cars speeding through the afternoon sunlight, filled with armed men, on their mission of death, all heading in our direction. It wasn't a pleasant image.

Each individual minute seemed to drag its feet. Each time a car drove past in the street below I'd jerk back, gripping the .38 tightly in my fist. I knew Dawn was feeling the same way. But she'd made her decision and I admired her for it. She was certainly some woman to have around when the chips were down.

Then, from the edge of my vision, I spotted the black car heading along the street at high speed. It pulled up just in front of the building. There were two guys in it. One got out and stood on the sidewalk gazing up at the side of the building. The driver stayed where he was, behind the wheel.

'It looks as though we're about to have visitors, Dawn,' I said tautly.

She edged over and stood beside me, looking down over my shoulder. 'You think they're Harry Grenville's men?' she asked in a low, but steady, voice.

'Impossible to be absolutely sure,' I replied. There was nothing to mark them out from any other guy you'd meet on the street. I realized that that was not strictly true. There was a look of efficient determination about that but that would apply to both the Feds and Corso's men.

After a few moments, the man walked towards the entrance and disappeared from sight. His companion got out of the car and stood beside it, looking intently in all directions. He had his right hand inside his jacket. Maybe he was feeling for a pack of cigarettes or, more likely, there was a gun concealed there.

I pulled Dawn away from the window and we stood behind the desk, waiting. I had the .38 trained on the door. Beside me, Dawn did likewise and I could see that the hand that held the Luger was as steady as a rock.

The loud knock on the door, when it came, made us both jump. 'Come in.' I called harshly.

The door opened and this guy came in. If he'd had a gun in his hand there'd have been at least a couple of slugs in him before he'd taken a couple of steps. But there wasn't. He held up his identification in his right hand.

'Peter Kendall, Federal agent.' he said crisply. 'Codeword Henning.'

Slowly, I lowered the gun; then pushed it back into its holster as he advanced into the room.

'We got word from Harry Grenville at Headquarters that you have some vital evidence concerning a racketeer named Al Corso.'

'That's right.' I picked up the diary from the desk and handed it to him. 'You'll find the entry for March twenty-ninth particularly interesting. There he describes how he tortured and then murdered another hoodlum named Jack Mortillo and dropped his body into the sea. It's all there in his own delicate handwriting.'

Kendall flipped through the pages until he came to the one in question. He ran his gaze down it, lips pursed. His expression didn't change but I knew he was impressed. Finally, he said, 'There's enough here to convict Corso of first degree murder and send him to the chair. Not even a dozen smart lawyers are going to get him off the hook this time.'

Closing the diary, he slipped it into his pocket. 'You've done a lot of good work, Johnny,' he said warmly. 'The Bureau owes you a whole heap of thanks.'

'Don't thank me,' I replied. He looked momentarily surprised. 'Somewhere out there is a little guy who risked a hell of a lot to get hold of that information.'

6

Corso's end

Dawn gave the Luger back to me. I squeezed her hand for a moment and then sat down, motioning Kendall to the chair in front of the desk. 'What happens now?' I asked.

'If I might use your phone, I'd like to get in touch with Grenville right away.'

'Sure. Go ahead.' I pushed the phone towards him. He rang the number, Grenville must have been waiting for the call, for after only a few seconds Kendall said. 'I've got everything, Harry. This is pure dynamite. It's all here in Corso's handwriting admitting to torture and murder.'

He spoke for several more minutes before putting the phone down. Then he gave a satisfied nod. 'I think I can promise you that Corso won't bother you, or anyone else again. He's being picked up as we speak. But as for the two of you, your lives are still in danger. The rest of the Organization won't forget what's happened and you, Johnny, will be at the top of their hit list.'

'I figured that,' I replied.

Kendall's face was grim. Turning to Dawn, standing quietly by her desk, he went on, 'Somehow I don't think they'll spare you either, Miss Grahame. We can get you into a protection programme but I have the feeling that neither of you will accept that.'

'Speaking for myself,' I said, 'I won't. I still have a case to finish. Getting Corso isn't the end of it.'

'The same goes for me too,' Dawn added.

Kendall sighed. 'Why do I get the feeling I knew you'd both say that?' He threw a swift glance around the office. 'One thing's for sure. You can't stay here and your place will be known to these people.' He looked directly at me as he spoke.

Dawn brushed a stray strand of hair from her forehead. 'They don't know where I live. We can hole up there until all this blows over.'

'Then if you're absolutely certain they've no idea where you live, Miss Grahame, I suggest you get there as quickly as possible and make sure you're not followed. This isn't going to be easy for you but I guess you've already considered that.

'The only thing in your favour is that Corso wasn't liked by most of the Organization. There were times when he went out of control, particularly when he was high on cocaine. There have also been rumours that several of the Big Boys, including Manzelli, wanted him out of the way. Mortillo had been marked for promotion by Rizzio.'

'That's a comfort,' I replied, trying to keep the sarcasm out of my voice. 'Just how do you know all of this.'

Kendall smiled. 'We have our methods. Now don't waste any time. Get going.'

We all went out and I locked the door behind us, wondering when I'd see the old place again — if ever. As Oliver Hardy often said: Henning, this is a fine mess you've gotten me into.

The two agents waited while Dawn and I got into my car. The street was still all but empty. There were three guys at the far corner but I had them taped for bums looking for a shakedown.

The relatively short drive back to Dawn's apartment was uneventful. As a precaution, I parked the Merc in a narrow alley well away from the place. Once back at the apartment, I checked all of the doors and windows.

Dawn watched me, following every movement. There was still that worried look in her eyes but she was bearing up well and trying desperately not to show the fear that must have been inside her.

While she made us a drink I tried to figure out what I could do next. It was some time since I felt like this, trapped and helpless. Having dragged Dawn into it made everything a thousand times worse. I knew how the Organization worked but she had very little idea of what could happen.

Handing me the drink she sat down on the couch beside me, crossing her legs.

Finally, she put into words the thoughts that were going through her mind.

'What do you think Rizzio and the others will do if they arrest Corso and try him for murder, Johnny?'

'I really don't know,' I told her truthfully. 'I saved Rizzio's neck once when the cops had him on the rack for Carlos Galecci's murder. That must count for something.'

I didn't tell her how Rizzio had acted when Corso had given the order for me to be taken for that ride. I had no wish to alarm her any more than she was already.

After she'd made us a meal we sat and talked. Every moment we waited for the door to burst open or a fusillade of shots to come through the window. When midnight came and nothing had happened, we figured that perhaps, for the time being, we were safe.

★   ★   ★

The next day it all came out. The radio was full of the news. The Feds had moved quickly and decisively. But Al Corso

146

would never stand trial for Jack Mortillo's murder or any others. When cornered, like the murderous rat he was, he decided to go out in a brief blaze of glory.

The moment when the Feds surrounded his place he knew the game was up. There was no more Mister Big Shot, no more chances for him to rely on the Organization to get him out of a mess, and nowhere for him to run. Two Federal agents were killed and three wounded in the gun battle that had ensued.

When they finally stormed the apartment they found him lying by the window with at least a dozen slugs in him. He evidently decided to live — and die — by the gun.

'So he's finally finished,' Dawn said soberly. 'I guess this means your case is closed.'

I shook my head. 'I wish it was but I'm afraid not, Dawn. It was Henning who hired me. Although he's probably sunning himself in Mexico now, there are still three bodies to account for and at least two of them are tied in with him. Somewhere out there a killer is on the loose and I mean to find him.'

'Then you don't think it was Henning who did those killings?' Dawn asked. 'After all, he always seemed to vanish before you found them.'

I finished the bacon and eggs she'd rustled up for breakfast and shook my head. I'd no proof that the little guy wasn't responsible for the murders — just a gut feeling in the pit of my stomach. But it was a feeling I'd had before and it had always proved me to be right.

Dawn carried the plates to the sink and came back with the coffee. 'Even if you're right, how are you going to go about it? Grenville warned us to stay out of sight.'

'O.K.,' I said. 'So things are going to be a bit difficult.'

'A bit difficult!' She had that exasperated expression on her face again. 'They're going to be downright dangerous, if not fatal.'

'I know. But we can't stay cooped up in here forever. And I'm not sure that this place is as safe as Kendall believes. Someone is sure to know where you live and I've no doubt that O'Leary can soon find us.'

I could almost feel the hands of my watch grinding around the face. The sensation of helplessness I'd experienced the night before had returned but it was stronger now. I'd never been in this situation before, except for the three years I'd spent in San Quentin, incarcerated inside four walls.

I was about to say something more when the phone rang. We both looked at it, wondering who the hell might be trying to get in touch with Dawn.

'Do you think I ought to answer it?' she asked in a low whisper.

I thought fast. I knew it wouldn't be either of those two agents. On the other hand it might be Harry Grenville with further instructions. I made up my mind, nodding, 'Better see who it is.'

Dawn picked up the phone. I could see her hand trembling slightly as she held it to her ear. 'Hello.'

She listened for a moment, her expression growing more frightened by the second. Then she held out the phone to me.

'Who is it?' I mouthed the words.

She placed her hand over the receiver. 'I don't know. It's a man. He says he knows you're here and it's important he should speak to you.'

I took the phone from her. 'Who is this?' I asked hoarsely. That little finger of ice was running up and down my back, sending a shiver through me.

A voice I didn't recognize said, 'There's a car waiting for you outside, Merak. If you know what's good for you, you'll get in it — Now!'

With a soft click, the line went dead.

'Who was it?' Dawn tried to look unafraid but failed.

Without answering I went over to the window, pulled the thick curtain aside slightly and looked through the narrow gap. Like the man on the phone had said there was a big black limousine standing patiently at the kerb. There were two men in it, both anonymous figures wearing dark coats.

I never forget a face and I'd seen these men before, knew immediately who their boss was.

Without looking round at Dawn, I said with as much confidence as I could muster, 'It's Manzelli. Evidently he wants to see me and he's sent transport and a couple of bruisers to see I get there safely.'

'Manzelli.' She uttered the single word in a frightened whisper. 'You're not going, are you? You'll be going to your death if you do.'

I pressed my lips together. 'Nobody turns down an invitation to visit Manzelli. Besides, somehow I don't think he wants me dead.'

'How can you say that, Johnny, after what's just happened to Corso. He'll know you've had a big hand in that.'

'Sure he will,' I agreed. 'But sending for me like this means he wants to talk. When Manzelli wants you dead, the first thing you know about it is when you find yourself staring down the barrel of a gun.'

I jammed my hat onto my head and made for the door. Before opening it, I said, 'Just stay here with the door locked, Dawn. You've still got the Luger if anything happens but somehow I don't think it will. Not until Manzelli's said what's on his mind.'

'Take care, Johnny.' She came up to me and kissed me full on the lips, holding me as if she never wanted to let me go. 'And don't worry about me. I know how to take care of myself.'

'I'm sure you do.' I opened the door and stepped outside.

The moment I did so, the guy in the back of the car opened the door and got out. He held the door for me, which was nice of him. I seldom got this treatment from members of the Organization.

Closing the door after me, the other went around and got in the other side. 'I guess you know where you're going,' he said, almost conversationally.

I nodded. 'Manzelli's.'

He grinned. 'Now you're catching on.'

We moved away from the sidewalk. Glancing over my shoulder, the last glimpse I had of Dawn was a slender figure standing at the window, one hand lifted. I wondered if I'd ever live to see her again.

The drive out into the country where

Manzelli lived took only twenty minutes. It was the smoothest ride I'd ever taken. At times it was as if the car were standing still and the road beneath it was moving beneath us.

This time, when we arrived, there was another nice touch. My companion led me to the front entrance. On every previous occasion I'd been here, it had been the tradesmen's entrance at the back. That made me think. Was this a case of nothing was too good for the lamb being led to the slaughter — or had I suddenly gone up in Manzelli's estimation? I knew, as we went inside, that I was soon going to find out.

My silent chaperone led me along a couple of corridors and then paused in front of a large door. It was a weird feeling, standing there not knowing what lay in wait for me on the other side.

He knocked twice, waited for a moment, then opened the door and motioned me inside. The door closed softly behind me. I knew without turning my head that the bruiser hadn't come in with me. I was alone in the big room, alone except for the grossly corpulent man who sat in the large, high-backed chair at the long table.

I knew him from the last two occasions when I'd been summoned here.

Enrico Manzelli, the Big Boss, the man who ran all of the outfits in L.A.

'Please come in, Mister Merak,' he said. His voice was remarkably soft for such a huge figure. 'Sit down.'

There were three empty chairs at the table directly opposite him. With a slight movement of his right hand, he indicated the middle one.

I sat down, wondering what was about to happen. It was patently obvious he was expecting two more visitors.

He sat watching me closely, his small eyes almost lost in the folds of flesh. I could feel them drilling right through me until they seemed to be scratching my back.

Placing the tips of his fingers together, he continued to scrutinize me in silence. If it was intended to make me feel uncomfortable, he certainly succeeded. I could imagine him at Alcatraz, standing looking at the guy in the chair, his hand on the switch, waiting to throw it.

Finally, he said smoothly, 'You're possibly wondering why I sent for you.'

'The thought had crossed my mind,' I replied.

The coarse flesh of his face rippled into something like a smile. 'Of course. Naturally you're curious. Before my other guests arrive I need to know certain things and I'm sure your answers are going to satisfy my curiosity.'

In spite of the apparent geniality of his words I knew that if I didn't give him the answers he wanted to hear I wouldn't be walking out of that door again.

'What is it you want to know?' I asked.

'That's better.' He gave the impression that he leaned back in the chair but because of his bulk it was impossible to be sure he had moved at all. 'Now we understand each other.

'Certain events have happened recently which are extremely worrying. It has, for example, come to my attention that you have been contacted by a man named Henning. Is that true?'

'Yes.'

Manzelli began tapping the table with his stubby fingers. For a moment he seemed to be lost in thought and with this man thoughts moved very slowly, but relentlessly, through his mind.

'Henning.' He repeated the name to himself. I knew it was one he was familiar with. His mind was like a photographic plate with every possible scrap of data imprinted indelibly upon it. Ten years from now he could recall every little detail of this meeting. 'A petty thief but one who was useful in certain ways.' He lowered his gaze. 'Do you know where this man is now, Merak?'

I shook my head. 'He has a peculiar talent for disappearing and leaving dead men behind.'

I knew I was telling Manzelli something he already knew but I figured he might know a little more about this strange business than I did.

'My first belief,' he went on after a long pause, 'was that Henning is this killer. But now I'm not at all certain. Had it been some other outfit with a grudge against

Rizzio my instinct tells me they would have used a gun.'

'So you don't believe that now?'

I wasn't sure if he would answer but after a momentary hesitation, he did. 'No. I believe there is someone else out there killing these men and, as you can appreciate, that is something I require to be rectified as quickly as possible. That is the main reason I summoned you here.'

I sat back in the chair breathing a faint sigh of relief. So far, Corso's name had never been mentioned. If, as I now hoped, Manzelli wanted me to find this mysterious killer, I was off the hook. Only temporarily, perhaps, but it was enough to make me feel a little better. When the man sitting in front of me gave an order, whether it was to a bum on the streets or a high-flying politician, it was obeyed without question.

Without elaborating on what he had just said, Manzelli put his left hand beneath the table. I guessed there was some kind of communication device there for a moment later, the door opened and the big guy came in.

157

'I'll see our two guests now,' he said. 'Show them in.'

I sat forward in the chair and waited. A few moments later, two men came into the room. I experienced a sudden shock of surprise at the sight of them, recognizing both at once. Sam Rizzio and Joe Malloy, the heads of two of the largest outfits in the city.

'Sit down, gentlemen,' Manzelli said in a low voice. He waved a hand towards the chairs on either side of me.

Malloy said nothing as he lowered himself into the chair on my left. Rizzio, however, said harshly, 'What the hell is Merak doing here?'

There was no change in Manzelli's tone as he said, 'He's here because I sent for him, Sam. I'm fully aware that he's been working with the FBI and is wholly responsible for what happened to Corso.'

'Then why — ?' Rizzio began; then fell silent as Manzelli held up a hand.

'Although he may not be aware of it, Merak did me a great service when he rid the Organization of Corso. I do not fully agree with his method but it served its purpose and saved me the trouble of having him eliminated.' He swung his glance to Malloy, 'Don't you agree, Joe?'

'Whatever you say.' Malloy's face was expressionless. 'The punk meant nothing but trouble as far as I'm concerned.' He looked across me at Rizzio. 'My guess is that he was responsible for me losing three of my best men in the Bandolero.'

Manzelli nodded. The thick flesh below his chin made even this gesture difficult.

'What do you say to that, Sam? Was Corso behind what happened there?'

For a moment, Rizzio seemed at a loss for words. I knew these two men hated each other like poison. Then he shrugged. 'Not to my knowledge. But I will admit that Corso was becoming something of a problem and I knew nothing about him being directly responsible for Mortillo's death.'

'Of course.' Whether Manzelli believed him or not it was impossible to tell from his expression. 'However, all of that is in the past. We now come to the reason I've called all three of you together. I'm fully aware that Merak here is working with the

159

Feds and that you, Sam, have put out a hit on him. I'm not condoning what he's done but unfortunately, in the circumstances we now find ourselves, I need someone to find this killer who's either working alone or with Henning and — '
He made a sharp gesture with his hand as Rizzio made to interrupt, 'in my mind he's the only one capable of doing this.

'Merak is under my protection — at least for the time being and until I give orders to the contrary. Is that clearly understood?'

Both men hesitated. I knew they didn't like this but they had no choice in the matter. If either of them stepped out of line the consequences would be far from pleasant for them both. After a pause, they both nodded reluctantly.

'Good. If he should need any help from either of you, you'll give it.'

Sitting there between two of the most powerful men in the Organization, I suddenly felt like a guy who'd stood in front of the gates of hell and then been told his time wasn't up and to go back. I'd never believed in miracles but at that moment I felt I'd just witnessed one.

Manzelli sat in silence for a few moments. Then he slid his hand beneath the table once more. 'You can all go now,' he said quietly. 'All except you, Merak.'

It was over. I remained seated as Rizzio left, closely followed by Malloy. At the door the bruiser stood waiting. He didn't even glance at Rizzio and Malloy as they pushed past him. He was waiting for Manzelli to finish with me and then escort me back to town.

'As I said earlier, this petty thief Henning appears to the key to this case,' Manzelli said. 'Find him and you may get the answers to a lot of questions.'

'That isn't going to be easy,' I told him. 'No one seems to know where he is. The last I heard from him he intended to slip out of L.A. and head for Mexico.'

Manzelli pursed his thick lips. 'I can tell you one thing. Henning is not m Mexico. It's true he had a small private plane waiting to take him there but he never made it — fortunately for him.'

'I don't understand.'

'The police had that possibility figured

out and were on to him. They had a cordon around the airport, so tight not even a rat could get through. He came back into town and that plane left without him. As I said, it was lucky for him he never got on it. Reports say it mysteriously exploded over the sea.'

That was news to me and it put a very different slant on things. There was no doubt in my mind the bomb had been put there to get rid of Henning. But it seemed that once again Lady Luck had smiled on him or there had been some kind of divine intervention looking after him.

'So he's still somewhere in town.'

'I believe so. Wherever he is the police have been unable to track him down. There is, however, one further small piece of information I can give you. In addition to his apartment in the city, he has a small place some thirty miles out in the desert.'

'Do you know exactly where it is?' I asked.

He shook his head ponderously. 'No. But I'm sure that a man of your ingenuity should have little difficulty locating it.'

I had the feeling that his implicit faith in my ingenuity was misplaced but I said nothing.

After a pause, he said, 'That is all for now. You may go now, Mister Merak.'

I got up. Halfway to the door, I paused and said, 'If I find out anything, do I get in touch with you?'

He shook his head again. 'No one gets in touch with me as you put it. Someone will contact you on a regular basis and you will inform them of any progress you make.' A pause, then, 'Goodbye, Mister Merak.'

Outside, the limousine was waiting for me, the driver sitting behind the wheel. Rizzio and Malloy had already left.

Getting into the car, I sat back against the plush seat. Those little mice were still scurrying around in circles inside my mind but for the time being I ignored them. There was only one thought uppermost in my mind. By some miracle I was off the hook.

I didn't doubt both Rizzio and Malloy would obey Manzelli's orders to the letter. I still had problems but these were the kind I encountered on an everyday basis. The first thing I had to do was follow up the information Manzelli had given me concerning the possible whereabouts of this guy Henning.

Half an hour later we pulled up in front of Dawn's apartment. I got out of the car, waited until it had disappeared, and then went to the door. She had evidently been watching for me. It opened at once.

'Oh God, Johnny, I thought you'd never come back.'

We went inside and I noticed she locked the door behind us, sliding the bolt into place.

'What happened with Manzelli?' she asked anxiously.

'Just get me a drink, Dawn, and then I'll tell you.'

As I sipped the bourbon, I recounted everything that had occurred. She listened carefully, following every word, a look of growing relief on her face.

When I'd finished, she said, 'So those hoodlums are not after you but you've still got to follow this case.'

I nodded, feeling the liquor bring back a cosy, warm feeling into my body. 'That's the deal. I don't know how O'Leary is going to take it but right now I don't give a damn.'

'And Harry Grenville? What about him?'

'Harry's got what he wanted. All he was after was Corso.'

I watched her as she went about the room moving the small ornaments on the mantelpiece. I figured she was still trying to take in this unexpected turn of events. Then she crossed to the window, looking out as if to convince herself that this was real and there was no one outside watching the place.

Turning with her hands clasped behind her back, she asked, 'How do you intend to start, Johnny?'

I glanced at my watch. It was a little after noon. 'I was figuring on driving out to see if I can find this place of Henning's in the desert. Manzelli said it's about thirty miles away.'

'The desert is a really big place, Johnny. It'll be like looking for a drop in the ocean.'

'That's true. I think I should first go back to the office. I have a map of the roads in that area. 'Perhaps that might give me a clue or at least narrow down the possibilities a little.'

'I'll come with you. Now we're in the clear I want to get out of this place for a while.'

I knew she wouldn't take no for an answer and twenty minutes later I was seated back in my old chair behind the office desk. Rummaging around inside the desk drawer I finally found the map I needed. Spreading it out in front of me, I studied it closely with Dawn peering down over my shoulder, one arm around my neck. I could feel her warm breath on my face and tried to concentrate on the job in hand. It wasn't easy.

After a few moments, she said, 'From what I can see there are only two passable roads into the desert from here.' She traced her finger across the map. 'I suppose if he really is out there it has to be one or the other.'

'Then there's only one thing to do,' I said. Taking a quarter from my pocket I held it in my hand. 'Heads we take this one.' I jabbed at the map with my forefinger. 'And tails we take the other.'

I spun the coin into the air, caught it and slapped it down onto the back of my hand. 'It's tails,' I said shortly. 'That's the road we'll try.'

★   ★   ★

Half an hour later we left the city behind us and it was then that the blistering heat of the desert really hit us. Even with all of the windows down, the hot wind seared our faces. In front of us, the narrow road seemed to stretch away to infinity.

It was going to be a long and uncomfortable drive.

This was the empty country. Nothing to be seen for miles except arid ground and the narrow ribbon of the road going seemingly nowhere.

I loosened the neck of my shirt. The sun was past its zenith but the vicious glare was everywhere. Dawn tried to settle herself against the window, her eyes narrowed as she scanned the surrounding terrain for any sign of the place Manzelli had

'So you think Manzelli was telling you the truth when he spoke of this place?' she asked. 'Why would anyone want to live out here in the middle of this wilderness?'

'Maybe Henning is one of those guys who like the solitude.'

'Solitude! God, Johnny, this is the nearest place to hell I can imagine.'

She lapsed into silence. Even the effort of talking was too much in that overpowering heat. Soon my eyes were beginning to ache from the endless strain of trying to see through the almost intolerable brightness.

Dawn was so quiet I thought she'd fallen asleep but with a suddenness that took me by surprise, she abruptly sat forward and pointed.

'There. Do you see it, Johnny?'

I slowed the car to a crawl and stared in the direction of her pointing finger. There was something there, a dark shape that stood out like a blot on the landscape against all of the surrounding emptiness.

Here there were small, stunted bushes thrusting brittle branches out of the dry ground as if they weren't enjoying growing where they were. I swung the Merc off the narrow highway onto the uneven ground.

'This isn't going to be pleasant,' I said, gritting my teeth as the car threatened to spin out of control on the soft earth. It wasn't. We were both thrown from side to side as I fought to keep the vehicle on a straight path.

As we drew closer I made out a small wooden building. It stood alone as if someone had just tossed it into the air and left it where it fell. We drew up in front of the door.

Letting her glance rove over it, Dawn said hoarsely, 'From what I can see this must be the ideal place for anyone who doesn't want to be found.'

I nodded. She was right. It was not too far from the highway but from inside it, one could see for miles in every direction. It would be impossible for anyone to approach it without being spotted long before they got there.

Dawn made to open the door and get out but I caught her arm and pulled her back. 'Be careful.' I warned. 'If Henning is in there he might not want company and it's highly likely he's armed.'

There were two windows, one on either side of the door and through the dusty windscreen I watched them closely. Curtains covered both of them but there was no sign of any movement, no hint that someone was watching us.

After a couple of minutes I made up my mind. We'd find out nothing just sitting there soaking in the heat.

'Wait here,' I said. I slipped the .38 from its holster and opened the car door. There was still no indication of life behind those windows. Walking up to the door, I knocked loudly and called, 'If you're in there, Henning, open up. This is Johnny Merak. I have to talk to you.'

There was no answer. In a funny sort of way I hadn't expected to find Henning here. If he'd been at home I was quite sure there would have been a warning shot fired, telling us we were not welcome. I tried the door. It was open.

That was when warning bells started sounding in my mind. I decided to check all the way around the house before entering. Very slowly I moved around the side. There was another single window at the rear but no door. A bin almost full of rubbish stood against the wall.

I went back to the front. Dawn was still seated inside the car. Pushing the door open, I held the .38 ready. As I'd guessed, the place was empty. There was only one room and no place to hide. The air inside was chokingly hot, burning my throat with every breath I took.

Putting the gun back in its holster, I went to the small table. A sudden sound brought me whirling round but it was only Dawn standing in the doorway.

'Looks as though there's nobody home,' I told her.

'So I see.' She pointed. 'Don't you think that's odd?'

I looked down and saw immediately what she meant. The small table was set for two. There was a coffee pot in the middle, half-empty. Clearly two people had been here preparing to have a meal. I felt the coffee pot. It was cold.

'I'd say this place has been used quite often but not for quite a while,' Dawn said. 'But what puzzles me most is — who was here with Henning? My impression of him when he came to the office was that he's a loner. He doesn't like the company of other people.'

'I got the same impression,' I agreed.

'So who is the visitor he's been entertaining?' Dawn asked over her shoulder as she walked slowly around the room.

'That's something I'd like to know. There'd been this nagging little thought at the back of my mind for some time now. All of these odd events that have happened weren't the work of one man. There must have been at least two of them working in cahoots.

'Even if Henning spirited himself away each time, it needed someone else to bring in those two bodies we found. And something tells me this mysterious other person is the killer we're looking for.'

I stared down at the two sets of dishes and cutlery laid out on the table. Some of the little bits of the jigsaw were beginning to sit but there was still a big hole in the middle and without that being filled in the picture would remain incomplete.

After a moment, I said, 'I suppose we should take a look around now that we've come all this way.' I didn't expect to find much of importance. Henning was far too clever to leave any real clues behind.

While Dawn went through the cupboards, I examined the contents of the drawers. Most were filled with papers stacked neatly together. A quick glance through them told me that the majority were to do with his work for Rizzio and the late lamented Al Corso.

There was nothing incriminating among them, certainly nothing that would stand up in court against Rizzio. I hadn't really expected anything like that. Henning would never have left anything pertaining to any illegal activities lying around in this place. The fact that he wasn't here and the door had been open testified to that.

Yet those little mice were never still. Now they were telling me that there was something here, something we were overlooking. Closing the final drawer, I straightened up and looked across at Dawn.

'Anything useful?' I asked.

She shook her head in obvious disappointment. 'Nothing — just some clothing, an old raincoat, and three pairs of shoes. What you'd expect to find in a man's wardrobe. The others contain only dishes and cutlery together with several tins of food. I don't think we're going to find anything here that will help us.'

'Maybe you're right.'

Inwardly, I knew that on this occasion, she wasn't. There was something wrong here, something that didn't quite click. Commonsense told me that Henning had to be somewhere close by otherwise he would have locked that door. Yet it was possible to see for miles around and there had been no sign of him — or his car.

I turned my attention back to the table. There was nothing out of the ordinary about the things on it but there was something on the floor under it. Bending, I picked it up. It was a ring; a gold signet ring. There were letters engraved on it but these were worn and difficult to make out.

'What's that?' Dawn asked. She came over as I held it up to the light.

I gave it to her and she studied it closely before saying. 'These letters look to me to be CLH. I'd say this must be Henning's ring. But how did it come to be here?'

'Obviously it didn't just fall off his finger,' I said, looking more closely at the carpet. Without looking up, I added, 'Just as I figured. There's been a struggle here. See how the carpet has been torn slightly. Those look like heel marks. My guess is that Henning was here, almost certainly asleep otherwise he would have spotted his attackers coming. But he did put up quite a fight before he was overpowered.'

Dawn looked at me wide-eyed. 'You think he's been killed like the others?'

'It's a definite possibility. After all, somebody tried to kill him when that plane exploded. Maybe this time they succeeded but somehow I doubt it. Whoever did this took their time, putting everything back in its place. If they just intended to kill him, they'd have left the body here. My guess is that nobody ever comes to this isolated spot. His body wouldn't be discovered for months, possibly years.'

She still seemed puzzled, however, spreading her hands in a gesture of incomprehension. 'Then why is everything laid out to give the impression there were two people here having a meal?'

'Unless you can get into the mind of this killer, I doubt if we'll get the answer to that,' I said.

After a final look around the room we left and drove back to the city. It had been a disappointing exercise. I'd hoped that Henning would be there and I might get some answers to the questions that were troubling me. Instead, the excursion had thrown up more questions.

Was Henning dead? Who had been out to that isolated place and either killed, or abducted him?

There was a car parked just outside my office when we arrived. It was one I recognized at once.

An old model T Ford.

Charlie Forsythe was waiting just outside the office door. I wasn't too pleased to see him. I needed time to consider what we had found that afternoon.

'At last, Johnny,' he said, grinning. 'I've been trying to get in touch with you for more than two days. Somehow I didn't think you were out of town.'

I unlocked the door and stood on one side for him to enter. He brushed past me and sat down.

Giving Dawn an oblique glance as she arched her eyebrows at me, I closed the door and placed my hat on the peg.

'So what can I do for you, Charlie?' I asked, sinking into my chair and eyeing him across the desk. 'Clearly you've got something important on your mind.'

He leaned back, staring at me through the thick lenses. 'You know me, Johnny. Always on the look out for news, especially anything connected with the Mobs. Somehow I think you've got a pretty good story to tell.'

'About what?' I asked.

'Why, about what happened to Corso,

of course. So far there's been no news as to how the Feds got anything on him that would stick. Besides, there have been rumours that you'd been declared persona non gratis by Rizzio and Malloy.'

'Now where did you get that from?' I asked tersely.

'I have my sources,' he said airily.

'I'm sure you have. But sometimes they can be wrong. As you can see I'm still upright and walking on my own two feet. And I can assure you that my relations with both of those guys are exactly as they were before.'

He raised his brows at that. 'Then my guess is that someone has made them change their mind. Would that someone be Manzelli?'

When I didn't answer him, he went on, 'This is off the record, Johnny. Has Manzelli okayed you and warned Rizzio and Malloy off?'

'All right, Charlie — he has. But you keep that out of your paper.'

'I will,' he promised.

'Then that's about as much as I can tell you at the moment and right now I'm particularly busy. I'll see you in a couple of days. If anything more turns up I'll see to it that you get it first.'

He seemed reluctant to leave but finally he got up and moved towards the door. There was a curious expression in his eyes as he said, 'I'll be seeing you, Johnny. You, too, Miss Grahame.'

When he'd gone Dawn said. 'Do you think he knows you've been to see Manzelli?'

'I'm sure he does. What's more, I think he also knows we've been out to Henning's place — and that worries me.'

7

The blue chevrolet

Two days passed and I was no closer to finding Henning — or, as seemed more likely, receiving news that his body had been found somewhere. I had the unshakable conviction that events were happening about which I knew absolutely nothing and that rankled.

If O'Leary was following any new leads on the two hoodlums who had been murdered he was keeping it quiet and not sharing that information with me.

Then I got a lucky break.

It was a little after seven in the evening and I was sitting at the bar in Mancini's. Kolowinski wasn't in his usual place. Then, in the mirror behind the counter I saw him come in. He noticed me at once, hesitated, and half turned as if to walk out.

Then he made up his mind and came

over, seating himself on the stool next to mine. Before he could say anything I signalled to the bartender who sidled over.

'What will it be?' he asked.

'Bring him the usual,' I said. 'I'm buying.'

When the drink came, Kolowinski downed half of it in a single swallow. Without turning his head he spoke out of the corner of his mouth. 'Everyone at the precinct figured you'd be dead by now, Johnny, after what happened to Corso. There was talk that Rizzio had put out a hit on you.'

I grinned. 'That's all it was, Jack, just talk. I guess I've got more lives than the proverbial cat though I'll bet there are quite a few folk would like to see me dead. O'Leary for one.'

'Don't be too hard on him, Johnny. He's a good cop just trying to do his job.'

'Maybe so. But he doesn't seem to be getting very far with this case.'

He finished his drink and I ordered him another. He sat with his fingers around it for a while. He had something

181

on his mind but seemed afraid to spit it out. At last, however, he said soberly, 'Who was it got you off the hook, Johnny? Manzelli?'

'Now why should you say that?' I asked, watching him closely.

He shrugged. 'Just a wild guess, I suppose. But I can't think of anyone else with enough pull to clamp down on a top guy like Rizzio.'

'O.K. So it was Manzelli,' I replied. 'But I was in such a deep hole after providing the FBI with enough evidence to get Corso into the chair I'd have accepted help from the Devil if it had been offered.'

I knew Kolowinski well enough to be certain that this information would go no further. I also knew from the look on his face that there was something more on his mind — something more important than my association with the Big Boss. He seemed to be struggling with his conscience.

'Is there something I should know, Jack?' I asked as he remained silent.

He licked his lips, then leaned sideways

until his face was right up to mine. 'I think you might like to go to forty-nine Burbank Street as soon as you can. I'm off duty at the moment and I'm saying no more. If you repeat this to anyone, I'll deny it.'

I didn't know what he meant but I finished my drink in a hurry and got up. 'Thanks, Jack. I never heard that last bit.'

I went out and a moment later I'd guided the Merc into the stream of traffic and was heading to Burbank Street.

I got there fifteen minutes later, not knowing what to expect, to find the road closed. There were a couple of uniformed cops standing on the sidewalk and a small knot of onlookers. A couple of police cars were parked about fifty yards further on and more cops milling around.

As I walked up, one of the cops a couple of yards away stepped forward and spread his arms wide. 'Sorry sir,' he said firmly. His tone was polite but intimated that I'd better not argue with him. 'This street is closed for the time being.'

I took out my card and showed it to him. He perused it closely then gave it back. 'A private investigator. I'm afraid that still doesn't allow you in. This is a homicide scene.'

'Perhaps if you were to give my name to whoever's in charge. My guess is that it's Lieutenant O'Leary.'

'It is sir. But as you can see he's pretty busy at the moment.'

I guessed I'd never get past this guy. He was as solid as the Rock of Gibraltar.

As that moment, however, O'Leary came out of the door of the house. He spoke to one of the men standing outside and then turned his head in my direction. He saw me at once. Breaking off his conversation abruptly he walked towards me.

'Merak!' he said sharply. 'I figured you'd be somewhere in the vicinity. I want to see you.' He gave a nod to the stolid figure by my side. The cop gave me a funny look and then lifted the tape for me to step under.

'What is it this time, Lieutenant?' I asked. 'Another murder like before?'

'Not exactly.' His tone was so brittle you could have shattered it with an ice pick. 'There are two this time.'

He led the way. I thought he would go into the house he'd just come out of but instead, the turned into the narrow alley at the side. Here there were two more cops, a small guy in a white coat kneeling on the ground and two bodies lying there.

The little guy whom I took to be a doctor, pushed himself to his feet. He looked straight at O'Leary. 'Both the same, Lieutenant,' he said quietly. 'Killed by a single stab wound to the heart.'

Before the Lieutenant could say anything, I butted in. 'Would you say they were killed here — or stabbed someplace else and dumped in this alley?'

The doctor hesitated. He was watching O'Leary not me. He said harshly. 'Who is this guy, Lieutenant?'

'Just a nosy private investigator named Merak. It's okay, you can answer his question.'

'Very well. At the moment it's impossible to be absolutely certain. They've both been dead for not more than three hours.' He switched his glance in my direction. 'What makes you think they weren't killed here?'

'A couple of things,' I told him. 'Firstly my guess is that they're connected to the two other murders and we know they were killed elsewhere and secondly, there's not much blood on the ground around either of them. If they'd been killed here I'd have expected more.'

O'Leary bent and examined the ground near both bodies. Then he nodded. 'You're right, Merak,' he said grudgingly. He rubbed a hand across his chin. 'Do you know either of them?'

I studied their faces closely. Nondescript features that could belong to anyone. Yet there was something familiar about both of them but I couldn't put my finger on where I'd seen them before.

'I've seen both of them somewhere before but for the hell of me, Lieutenant, I can't remember where.'

'Well if it should come to you, you'll let me know at once. In the meantime we'll photograph them and then go through the rogues' gallery back at the precinct. If we can tie them in with the other two it'll be helpful.'

'You think these are all mob slayings?'

'That's the way it looks to me at the moment. And I'm quite sure we're dealing with the same killer.'

I agreed with him on that point. These were all professional slayings — the same killer, the same knife, the same odd MO of killing the victims in one place and then dumping them somewhere else.

That all appeared to be logical and straightforward. But there was an enigma. Where did Henning fit into all of this? He was the one who had somehow initiated this weird chain of events yet he seemed to come and go at will like some will-o'-the-wisp, as insubstantial as smoke.

'Have you questioned any of the neighbours?' I asked.

'Not much help there.' He pointed to the building next to the alley. 'This place is empty. Has been for the last couple of years. Nobody in any of the others along the street appear to have seen or heard anything.'

'Or they're afraid to say.'

He nodded grimly; then inclined his

head towards someone who had just come out of one of the houses. 'He might have more luck?'

It was Charlie Forsythe. I might have known he would be somewhere around if there was a story to be had. He spotted me and walked over.

'Have they brought you in on this, Johnny?' he asked.

Before I could reply, O'Leary snapped, 'No we haven't. This is strictly police business.' He glanced in my direction. 'I reckon he just happened to be passing by but since he's here he's making himself useful. Have you got anything?'

He shook his head. 'Not much, Lieutenant. People are usually willing to talk to reporters, maybe hoping to get their names in the papers. But these folk have just clammed up. My guess is they've been warned off.'

He pushed his spectacles more firmly onto his nose. 'I did get one guy to open up a bit, however. He says there was a dark blue Chevrolet came along this street and he's pretty sure it turned into this alley. He never saw it come back so he reckons it must have driven straight on.'

He pointed his pen along the alley. 'There's a road cuts across about three hundred yards away.'

'When was this?' O'Leary asked.

'He reckons it was between two and three hours ago.'

'Where is this guy now?' I asked.

Forsythe pointed towards the opposite sidewalk. 'That's him. He's not very talkative. I can't say I blame him, witnessing a possible murder.'

O'Leary made to accompany me across the street but at that moment, one of the officers called to him. I was glad of the interruption. From what Forsythe had said, it seemed that most of the folk didn't like talking to cops.

The guy seemed on the point of walking away but stopped when I called to him. 'I want to ask you a couple of things about this car you saw,' I told him. I took a ten-spot from my wallet and held it out where he could see it.

He looked like a typical bum and there was an oddly vacant expression on his face. I wasn't sure I could place much reliance on what he said but it might be the only lead I'd get.

His eyes followed the bill in my hand as I went on, 'Did you get a good look at the passengers in that car you saw?'

'Are you an undercover cop?' His words were slightly slurred. I couldn't smell any alcohol on him so I figured he had some kind of affliction.

'No. I'm a private detective. I'm following up a case and those two stiffs back there might be connected with it.'

He hesitated, still unsure of me. Then he reached out a hand that shook a little and grabbed the ten dollars. 'Yeah, I saw them. I couldn't recognize any of them again if that's what you want to know.'

'Can you tell me how many there were?'

'Four.'

'You're sure about that?'

He nodded. 'I don't know if the driver was drunk but they were weaving all over the road. They almost hit me as they went past. There were two men in the back. I guess they were really plastered.'

'What makes you say that?'

'The way they were sitting. Slumped forward as if they couldn't sit up straight.'

'Anything else you noticed?'

'Yeah. The little guy sitting beside the driver.'

'What about him?'

'He wore these thick glasses and there was something else.'

'What was that?'

His glance was fixed on the wallet I still held in my hand. He was almost drooling at the sight of it. I took out another ten-dollar bill and thrust it into his hand. 'What was it you saw?' I asked again.

He lifted his head and threw a wary glance towards the cops on the other side of the street. Then he muttered in a low voice. 'He had a gun in his hand. He was pointing it at the driver's head. That's when I took off in a hurry. I figured it was no business of mine.'

I turned on my heel and left him. By the time I reached the opposite sidewalk he had disappeared.

O'Leary came over. 'Did you get any more out of him?' he demanded.

'Only that there were four people in that car. The two sitting in the back were slumped forward in their seats. He thought they were drunk. My guess is they were dead.'

'That figures,' O'Leary said. 'Obviously they were these two guys. Whoever was in that car must've dumped them here and left.' He nodded and rubbed his eyes. He wasn't the fastest thinking cop on the force but he'd get there after a while.

'One other thing, Lieutenant,' I said after a brief pause. 'If these killings are following the same pattern, I reckon you'll find these are two more of Rizzio's men. If that's the case, he's going to be pretty sore and it's possible, in spite of what Manzelli might do to keep the peace, he'll start something.'

I looked around for Forsythe but there was no sign of him. My guess was he'd got as much information as he needed and had gone to write it up for the paper.

By now it was getting dark. I realized I'd had nothing substantial to eat since early morning and my stomach was beginning to protest. I'd noticed a small restaurant about a quarter of a mile back and decided to try for something there.

Parking immediately outside it, I went in. The place was only small but there was a surprising choice on the menu. I ordered a steak, potatoes, peas and carrots and then found myself a table in the corner furthest from the door.

It was a habit I'd cultivated over the years with the Mobs. Never have your back to the door and give yourself plenty of room just in case trouble should happen.

My meal came and with it — Forsythe. He sat down in the seat opposite.

'I thought I spotted you through the window,' he said without preamble. 'I'd like to talk to you.'

He called over to the counter for a couple of sandwiches and a beer, waited until they came, then went on, 'A little bird tells me that you and your secretary went out into the desert a couple of days ago.'

I tried to control the surprised look on my face. 'It seems you know quite a lot. Are you still following me?'

He shook his head and chewed on his sandwich. 'Not at all. I'm sure you know that your car is almost instantly recognizable all over L.A. It's just that one of my colleagues who was going on an assignment for the editor saw you heading in that direction.'

'So we took a trip into the desert. What's strange about that?'

'With the temperature close to the hundred mark? I'd say it had to be something more important than a pleasure trip.' His eyes were like gimlets.

'All right, Charlie, I'll level with you. I don't know what your interest is in Henning but whatever I tell you goes no further than these walls — for the time being.'

'I understand.' He nodded and the light from the streetlamp just outside the window flashed off his spectacles so that his eyes seemed to sparkle in the dimness with something more than just interest. 'I give you my word.'

'Very well. I received information from a very reliable source that Henning has a place out in the desert about thirty miles from here. Unfortunately, you'll under-stand that I can't divulge the name of this source.'

'Of course. And did you find this place?'

'Yes, we found it but when we got there it was empty and the door was open. There were, however, obvious signs of a struggle and the table had been set for two. Clearly he'd been expecting a visitor.'

'But there was nothing to tie him in with these murders?'

I shook my head. 'Nothing at all, I'm afraid. There were papers but all of these were simply records of work he did for Rizzio and Corso, dating back several years. All were perfectly legit.'

I finished my meal and pushed the empty plate away. Taking out my pack of cigarettes, I offered him one. When he shook his head I pushed one between my lips and lit it.

'It sounds to me like a wasted trip,' Forsythe observed.

'We did find one thing that might be of help. A ring. It was lying on the floor under the table. It must have dropped there during the struggle.'

Forsythe looked up sharply at that, his hand clasped tightly around his glass. As he sipped it slowly, peering at me over the rim, he said, 'Then it must be Henning's ring. A gold signet with his initials engraved on it?'

'I'd say it almost certainly was his.' I didn't mention that my earlier informant had told me that a guy closely resembling Henning had been seen in that car, holding a gun to the driver's head. After all, there were certain bits of information I preferred to keep to myself.

Finishing my cigarette, I stubbed it out in the ashtray and then got up. Looking down at Forsythe, I said crisply, 'Don't forget, all of that news about Henning's place is strictly between ourselves.'

'I won't forget.'

After paying for the meal, I went outside. It was completely dark now. The sky was perfectly clear and fortunately the temperature had dropped a little making it more bearable.

I'd only taken a couple of steps towards

my car when a hand gripped my arm and spun me round.

'Hey!' Somehow I got the word out. 'What the hell is this?'

The guy who had hold of me was almost seven feet in height making me feel like a dwarf beside him. He was built to match and his face was one only a mother could love. He looked like a prizefighter who'd been in one too many fights even down to the broken nose and cauliflower ears.

'The boss wants a word with you, punk.' His voice had the timbre of a chain saw slicing its way through a tree.

'There's no need to be so rough,' I said, wincing as the fingers gripped me more tightly. 'I'll talk to your boss without being hustled like this.'

'He said you might make trouble,' grated my companion, lifting me off my feet. He began hauling me along the sidewalk. A couple of passers-by stared curiously at us and then hurried on. Obviously they weren't going to get involved or make any comment to the man mountain at my side.

'I never make trouble,' I replied. 'Just let me walk on my own two feet.'

He was clearly no Einstein but something must have penetrated his thick skull for he relaxed his grip a little, lowering me so that my feet touched the sidewalk again.

He took me around the next corner where a sleek limousine stood waiting at the kerb. Apart from the man sitting motionless behind the wheel I could just make out the little guy in the back. His face was in deep shadow but I knew at once that it wasn't Malloy.

The door popped open and my new friend pushed me inside. The door closed with barely a whisper as I pushed myself upright in the seat. Turning my head, I stared at the man beside me. It was Sam Rizzio.

'I think it's time we had a talk, Merak,' he said almost casually. 'One without Manzelli or Malloy being present.'

'All right, Sam. What is it you want to talk about?'

'I think you know already. This man Henning.'

'You want to know something, Sam?' I said. I used his Christian name on purpose, knowing he wouldn't like it. 'I'm beginning to bitterly regret the day that Henning walked into my office. He's landed me in more trouble than any other client I've ever had. Even to the point of being taken out for a trip on the ocean.' I added the last bit to show him that I hadn't forgotten the way he'd given in to Corso and sent me out to almost certain death.

I saw him nod. He took an expensive cigar from his pocket. Whether he was feeling generous or it was to atone in some way for not stopping Corso issuing my death sentence I didn't know, but he offered me one.

We both lit up like two old pals meeting in some nightclub. Somehow I didn't think so.

'I regret that decision, Johnny. You've been useful to me several times in the past. But I hope you'll understand my position. I've lost four good men in almost as many days and something up here — ' He tapped his forehead meaningfully, ' — tells me that Henning is responsible.'

'Not Malloy or Corso?'

'No. Malloy's had three of his own men shot in the Bandolero. Corso was a ruthless killer and maybe he wanted my job but he didn't have the brains to do anything like that. Whoever is doing this is working alone and Henning is the one common denominator.

'I want him found — and fast. The cops don't seem to be doing anything. I've had my own men searching for him. But he's gone to ground somewhere and nobody seems to know where. Now Malloy, and perhaps Manzelli, believe that I'm using him to bump off Malloy's boys, hoping to start a gang war.'

'And are you?' I knew it was a dangerous question to ask but it was something I needed to know.

'Of course not. At the moment I'm quite satisfied with the territory I've got. I've no wish for any more. A gang war would help nobody.'

Oddly enough, I believed him.

'If I'm going to have any chance of

finding Henning I need to know more about him. I know he kept the books for you, carried out money transactions with the other outfits, but apart from this I know hardly anything.'

Rizzio blew smoke into the air. 'There's not much I know about him. I inherited him from Galecci. He was no killer but he was an expert with figures. When Corso came, he worked with him. He was someone who always stayed in the background not the usual type of guy you find in the Organization.'

'Do you know if he had any friends, really close friends?'

'None that I'm aware of although there was someone he used to meet on a fairly regular basis. This was after he started with Corso.'

'You've no idea who this friend of his was or when this — liaison — started?'

Rizzio stubbed out his cigar in the small silver ashtray in front of him. 'I'm fairly certain it began around the time that Jack Mortillo was killed.'

Jack Mortillo! I ran the name over in my mind. Was it possible, I wondered, that I'd been on the wrong track all the time?

'You've been a big help, Sam,' I said. 'Things are beginning to make sense now.' I opened the limousine door. 'There's something I have to do tomorrow. If I'm right, I may have your killer for you.'

8

Killer unmasked

It was still early the next morning when I parked my car in a small side street and walked to the imposing building on the corner of the intersection. The elevator wasn't working. I climbed the three floors to where the newspaper offices were located.

The graveyard shift would be almost finished but I hoped to catch one of the guys I knew before they all left for the day.

Jim Benton had helped me on several occasions, hunting out pieces of information, some of which had made front-page headlines while others had been tucked away inside the paper.

I found him in his small office, sitting back in his chair, his legs on the desk. Small and white haired, he'd collect his pension in a couple of years and retire to some little place he knew in South Carolina.

I knocked and went it. Taking his pipe from his mouth, he swung his legs to the floor. 'Come in, Johnny.' He waved his hand towards the chair near the desk. 'It's been a long time. I gather this isn't a social call.'

'Not exactly, Jim,' I said, dropping into the chair and stretching out my legs. 'I need some information on Jack Mortillo.'

He tapped his pipe out in the ashtray and began refilling it from a small pouch. 'How far back do you want to go with this guy?' he asked finally.

'Just a couple of years or so.'

Benton struck a match and waved the flame over the bowl of his pipe until he got it going to his satisfaction. Through the cloud of blue smoke, he said, 'There may be something on him in one of our recent editions. We ran the story of Corso's shootout with the Feds. You had a hand in that I believe.'

I nodded. I didn't want to go into all of that otherwise Benton would keep me talking until evening. 'I don't think I'll find what I want in any recent edition, Jim.'

'So what is it you want to know about Mortillo?' he asked.

'I'd like to find out the name of his wife before she married him.'

Benton stared at me, his mouth half open. 'Mortillo's wife? Why in tarnation do you want to know that? The guy's been dead for two years and she's probably married again.'

'Perhaps. This may be a long shot but I have this feeling that, somehow, she has a lot to do with a case I'm working on.'

'Fair enough, Johnny. If you'll come with me we'll see what we can dig up.' He got out of his chair, wincing a little as if the movement caused him some pain.

We went along a short corridor and into a large room. There were no windows and the place was dimly lit. Long shelves were filled with newspapers, some so yellow that they appeared to be a hundred years old.

'We haven't got around to putting them all on microfilm,' Benton explained. 'Once that's done it'll make things a lot easier and give us a hell of a lot more space.'

He indicated a stack of newspapers. 'If she's mentioned anywhere, Johnny, it'll be somewhere in there. Bring them through into my office, the light's better in there.'

I carried them through and put them down on the small table by the window. It looked as though I'd have at least two hours' work ahead of me. However, knowing the date when Mortillo had been killed proved a big help.

There were three editions all carrying the news of the finding of his body washed up onto the beach. There was also a picture of him on the front page of one of them. I studied it closely — a handsome looking guy with black wavy hair and brown eyes. I could guess from his picture that he was definitely a lady's man.

I read through everything there without finding any reference to his wife. I reckoned my best chance would be to find details of his funeral. As I remembered it, this had been a big affair even by the standards of the Organization. Most of the other gangs had been present to show their respect. How much was well intentioned and how many there had been glad to see him depart this life was something I didn't know.

Tilting the paper towards the light coming through the window, I scanned the list of those present. At first, I thought I was plumb out of luck. His wife was mentioned but only by her married name — Dolores Mortillo. That didn't help me at all.

Benton came over. He had his coat on and was evidently about to leave. 'Find anything important, Johnny?' he asked.

I leaned back in my chair and shook my head. 'Nothing of any help to me. Maybe this was just an idea I had that mean nothing.'

'Stick with it, Johnny. I've known y hunches in the past and they're us right. Besides, it's possible that — broke off as another thought struck

'I've just remembered. There m a quicker and easier way of find about her.'

'Oh, what's that?'

He glanced at his watch. 'Slim Madden. He knows more about the members of Rizzio's outfit than Rizzio himself. He investigated them all for some piece he was writing for the *Chicago Times*. Seems they've heard of our criminal fraternity even there. That was about a year ago. If anyone can give you the information you want, he's your man.'

'And where can I find this Slim Madden?'

'He should be here in about ten minutes. He's on the other shift. I'll wait and introduce him.'

The guy who came in ten minutes was taller than Benton but his ʾnced stoop made him look ʾ mass of grey hair gave him a ʾistinguished look. He had the ʾe eyes that took in every little ʾkoned that if he hadn't been ʾe'd have made a damned ʾe.

ʾfaʾduced us and, after taking ʾdden sat down at the table

ʾg for some information,

Mister Merak,' he said courteously. Evidently he was a reporter of the old school. 'What is it, exactly, that you wish to know?'

'You probably remember Jack Mortillo who was murdered by Al Corso two years ago,' I said.

'I remember him very well,' Madden acknowledged. 'A pity he chose that kind of life. He'd have made a good governor or senator if he'd chosen the straight and narrow. But I'm digressing. What do you want to know about him?'

'Not him,' I said. 'His wife.'

'Dolores Mortillo.'

'That's right. Do you know her maiden name before she married him?'

He pursed his lips. 'Certainly. Dolores Forsythe. She was some kind of showgirl before she met Mortillo.'

Despite the fact that I'd been half expecting it, I experienced a sense of shock. So here was the link I'd been searching for. It only needed one more piece of information for everything to drop neatly into place.

For the next quarter of an hour I sat in

Benton's office as Madden spilled everything about Jack Mortillo and his wife. The more he told me, the more sense everything made. It had required only two key pieces of information for the entire picture to be revealed.

Before I could give it all to O'Leary, however, I had to find Henning. I knew I'd failed on earlier occasions but this time I was convinced of where he was hiding. By now, he'd know that Dawn and I had been out to that small building in the desert. He might not expect me to go there again.

Using the phone on Benton's desk, I rang the one in my office. It burred twice and then Dawn answered.

'I won't be in for a little while, Dawn,' I told her. 'I think I've cracked this case. All I have to do now is find Henning and — '

'You know where he is?'

'I'm pretty certain he's out at that place in the desert. I'm going there now.'

A pause and then she said, 'Watch your step, Johnny. He may look harmless but I'd sooner trust a rattlesnake.'

'Don't worry. This time I'm taking

O'Leary with me.' I heard her faint sigh of relief and then put the phone down.

I expected the Lieutenant to tell me to go to hell when I rang him a couple of minutes later and asked him to meet me outside the precinct. When I told him I might be able to take him to where Henning was hiding out, however, he finally agreed.

★ ★ ★

In the mid-morning sunlight, the small house looked even more isolated than I remembered it. Turning off the narrow dusty track I gripped the wheel of the Merc tightly in both hands as we bumped over the uneven, rocky ground.

O'Leary had maintained a stiff-lipped silence all the way out from the city. Now he said harshly, 'Don't you think it might be easier on us if we got out and walked?'

'Easier, perhaps, Lieutenant,' I said in reply, 'but also easier to collect a bullet. If Henning is inside, I'm damned sure he's armed and he'll have seen us five minutes ago. Besides, I'd prefer it if he thinks it's just me coming. If we'd used a couple of squad cars, we'd have been met with a hail of bullets.'

'And what makes you think he might be here?' O'Leary gripped the dashboard as we hit a deep hollow.

'That car yonder, tucked away at the back of the place. It wasn't there when I was here last.'

I stopped the car two hundred yards from the front door. The blast of heat from the desert struck me like a physical blow as I got out. O'Leary came to stand beside me. Cupping his hands, he shouted, 'This is Lieutenant O'Leary of the LAPD. If you're in there Henning, come out with your hands raised where I can see them.'

There was no answer.

The place might have been empty as a tomb for all the reaction he got.

'We're going to have to prise him out, Lieutenant,' I said, taking out the .38. 'You take the front and I'll watch the back. Whatever happens, I need him alive.'

For a moment, I thought he was going

to argue. Then he must have figured that I knew Henning better than he did and said nothing. He pulled out his own gun and commenced to run forward, doubled-over, towards the front of the house.

I waited for a few seconds; then moved around towards the rear where Henning's car stood lazing in the sunlight. A couple of shots rang out as I flung myself down behind the car. I hoped that O'Leary hadn't stopped one.

There were more shots and then silence. I waited. I hoped that the Lieutenant hadn't been over-enthusiastic and killed Henning. That would spoil everything.

I was on the point of getting to my feet, ready to join O'Leary and rush the place, when a sudden noise reached me from close by. A moment later, the solitary window at the back of the house swung open.

Henning thrust one leg over the sill, turned, got both legs out and hung for a moment from the ledge before dropping to the ground. He still had a gun clutched tightly in his right hand.

I covered the distance between us in less than five seconds and rammed the muzzle of the .38 hard against his spine before he could turn.

'This is as far as you go, Henning,' I said softly. 'Now drop that gun.'

I reckon he knew when he was on a bad roll of the dice for he did as he was told. Picking up his gun, I marched him around to the front where O'Leary was still covering the house.

O'Leary took Henning's gun from me and put the cuffs on him, thrusting him unceremoniously into the back of the Merc. I got behind the wheel and turned the key in the ignition as the Lieutenant closed the rear door.

'Nice work, Johnny,' he said as I spun the car and headed back towards the narrow road. He even sounded as though he meant it. 'This just about wraps up the case as far as you're concerned.'

'There's just one favour I'd like to ask, Lieutenant,' I said.

'What's that?'

'I'd like you to bring Henning to my office in an hour. I've one more phone call to make and then I think it might be possible to unravel the whole mystery completely.'

I noticed his face in the rear mirror. He was trying to figure out just what I was up to and whether to agree. Finally, however, he nodded. 'All right, Merak. We'll both be there in an hour.'

★ ★ ★

An hour later I was sitting behind my desk while Dawn was just putting the coffee cups away.

O'Leary was the first to arrive. He had brought Kolowinski with him together with Henning. The little guy didn't look too good so I let him sit in the chair facing me. He slumped there with his cuffed hands in his lap not saying a word.

'All right, Merak,' the Lieutenant said sharply. 'I've brought Henning here as you asked but if this is just another stunt of yours, I'll — '

'Relax,' Lieutenant I said calmly.

He swallowed thickly as if my words had threatened to choke him. 'So what is it you want to see me about? And why Henning?'

'He's one of the central figures in all this,' I explained. 'But I'm also waiting for another arrival.'

O'Leary looked surprised. 'Another arrival?'

'That's right.' I glanced up as a sharp knock came on the door. 'This will be him, I guess.' I called out, 'Come in, Charlie.'

Forsythe came in. He glanced at the others in the office; then said with a sudden hardness in his tone, 'I thought you said you had a story for me, Johnny. What are all these people doing here?' His glance fell on the figure n the chair. 'So you've found Henning at last.'

'That's right.'

O'Leary stepped forward. His face had suddenly gone red, a sure sign that he was both angry and impatient. 'If you've got anything to say, Merak, get on with it. I'm booking Henning here on a charge of conspiracy to murder and I don't want you interfering in it.'

I leaned back and lit a cigarette. 'Very

well, Lieutenant. Some way into this strange case, I figured there had to be two people, working closely together. I knew one of them was Henning since he was always on the scene whenever anything happened.'

'And then he kept disappearing,' Kolowinski put in. 'We know all of that, Johnny.'

I nodded. 'Of course. But somehow I doubt if he could carry a dead guy into either the warehouse, or that room at the Bandolero unaided. There had to be someone else, someone even more deadly than Henning.

'But what threw me at the time was that I believed both of these guys had the same motive — greed, a lust for money. My guess was that that hundred grand Henning stole was just peanuts compared to what they finally hoped to grab from both Rizzio and Malloy.'

'So you're saying this wasn't their plan?' O'Leary seemed unable to take in what I was saying.

'Oh no, that wasn't their plan at all. It wasn't until I realized that they were working together but had two completely different motives that the clues started to fall into place. What Henning wanted more than anything else was power. You wouldn't think that, looking at him now.'

He certainly made a pathetic figure, sitting huddled in the chair, his face vacant, eyes staring at nothing in particular.

Continuing, I went on, 'He'd worked for years and never got the recognition or praise he thought he deserved. He wanted Rizzio out of the way so that he could take over as boss of the outfit.

'That tale he spun me about some blackmailer wanting dough to keep quiet was completely false. There was no one blackmailing him. In reality he needed a patsy to take the rap — someone to divert attention from himself. He chose me and made damned sure that eventually I got that information which enabled the FBI to take out Corso. So long as Al remained Rizzio's second in command, Henning had no chance of stepping into Rizzio's shoes.'

'And how was I supposed to get rid of

Rizzio?' Henning sneered, speaking up for the first time.

'You were systematically killing Rizzio's men and passing the word around that Rizzio was too weak to do anything about it — that the outfit needed a new boss, one who could get to the bottom of these murders.

'You reckoned you could swing most of them behind you. The fact that you'd stolen money from them right under their noses meant Rizzio hadn't a clue what was going on in the Organization.'

'And who is this second killer?' O'Leary demanded. 'You reckon you know?'

I didn't answer his question. Instead, I glanced across at Forsythe standing beside Sergeant Kolowinski. 'You're not writing any of this down in your notebook, Charlie,' I said smoothly. 'Is that because you know it all down to the very last detail?'

He must have seen something on my face that made him realize he'd been dealt a bad hand for, without warning, his right hand slid inside his jacket reaching for the gun I was sure was there.

He almost had it out when Kolowinski moved. His stiffened right hand slammed down hard on Forsythe's wrist. I heard the bone crack as the weapon dropped from his fingers.

'There's your other killer, Lieutenant,' I said. 'The guy who used the freedom of the press to find out exactly how the investigation was progressing. I'd guessed he placed that bomb on the aircraft that exploded over the sea. Henning, of course, never intended to take it. He knew beforehand what was to happen, hoping that everyone would believe he was dead.'

O'Leary nodded to Kolowinski. 'Cuff him, Sergeant.'

Forsythe flashed me an angry look. 'You seem to forget that it was me who saved your life when those hoodlums were about to send you to the bottom of the ocean.'

'Sure it was and I'll be eternally grateful to you, Charlie. But that wasn't done out of the goodness of your heart. The only reasons you did it were to throw me and the cops off the scent — and because you needed my connections with the FBI to finally pin Mortillo's murder on Corso.'

'You'll never be able to prove any of this,' Forsythe said, his voice shrill now that he was almost yelling the words.

I stubbed out my cigarette. 'Oh, I can prove it all right,' I said.

'But what motive did he have for joining up with Henning and killing Rizzio's men?' O'Leary asked.

'Oh his one burning intention was to see that Corso was killed. I had quite a long talk with a guy called Slim Madden. He did a lot of digging into Rizzio's bunch a couple of years ago.' I looked across at Forsythe. 'It must have hit you really bad when your sister's husband was murdered.'

'His sister's husband?' Dawn interrupted in a puzzled tone.

'That's right. She was married to Jack Mortillo and a couple of months after his murder she took her own life. That right, isn't it, Charlie? She stabbed herself through the heart with that knife you gave her as a present, years before. The same knife you used to kill your victims.'

'You'll never be able to prove any of this, that I've been working with Henning.' Forsythe's voice was becoming shriller now.

'No? You made two very big mistakes, Charlie. When you took me out in your car to exchange information you took off your spectacles to polish them.'

'So what does that prove?'

'It doesn't take a rocket scientist to recognize the difference between plain glass and a lens. Your eyesight is as good as mine. Secondly, when we told you about the ring we'd found in Henning's little hideout in the desert you immediately said it was Henning's with his initials engraved on it.

'Yet you'd told me that you didn't know Henning, that you'd never met him. How could you know it was his ring unless you were lying about not knowing him or you were there at the time?'

We do hope that you have enjoyed reading this large print book.

Did you know that all of our titles are available for purchase?

We publish a wide range of high quality large print books including:
Romances, Mysteries, Classics
General Fiction
Non Fiction and Westerns

Special interest titles available in large print are:
The Little Oxford Dictionary
Music Book, Song Book
Hymn Book, Service Book

Also available from us courtesy of Oxford University Press:
Young Readers' Dictionary
(large print edition)
Young Readers' Thesaurus
(large print edition)

For further information or a free brochure, please contact us at:
Ulverscroft Large Print Books Ltd.,
The Green, Bradgate Road, Anstey,
Leicester, LE7 7FU, England.
Tel: (00 44) **0116 236 4325**
Fax: (00 44) **0116 234 0205**

THE UNDEAD

John Glasby

On the lonely moor stood five ancient headstones, where a church pointed a spectral finger at the sky. There were those who'd been buried there for three centuries, people who had mingled with inexplicable things of the Dark. People like the de Ruys family, the last of whom had died three hundred years ago leaving the manor house deserted. Until Angela de Ruys came from America, claiming to be a descendant of the old family. Then the horror began . . .

CARLA'S REVENGE

Sydney J. Bounds

Society girl Carla Bowman is young, beautiful — and wild. She is the honey of King Logan, a gangster running a protection racket on New York's East Side, and she becomes caught up in violence and bloodshed. Carla double-crosses Logan and joins his rival, Sylvester Shapirro, only to become his captive in a sanatorium. She escapes, but when she learns that Shapirro has killed her father, Carla's only desire is to revenge her father's death — whatever the cost to herself . . .